G R JORDAN

The Death of Macleod

A Highlands and Islands Detective Thriller

Symbols are powerful because they are the visible signs of invisible realities.

SAINT AUGUSTINE

Contents

Foreword

The events of this book, while based on known areas in Scotland, are in an entirely fictional setting and all persons are entirely fictitious.

Acknowledgement

To Ken, Jessica, Jean, Colin, John and Rosemary for your work in bringing this novel to completion, your time and effort is deeply appreciated.

Novels by G R Jordan

The Highlands and Islands Detective series (Crime)

1. Water's Edge
2. The Bothy
3. The Horror Weekend
4. The Small Ferry
5. Dead at Third Man
6. The Pirate Club
7. A Personal Agenda
8. A Just Punishment
9. The Numerous Deaths of Santa Claus
10. Our Gated Community
11. The Satchel
12. Culhwch Alpha
13. Fair Market Value
14. The Coach Bomber
15. The Culling at Singing Sands
16. Where Justice Fails
17. The Cortado Club
18. Cleared to Die
19. Man Overboard!
20. Antisocial Behaviour
21. Rogues' Gallery
22. The Death of Macleod - Inferno Book 1

Kirsten Stewart Thrillers (Thriller)

The Contessa Munroe Mysteries (Cozy Mystery)

The Patrick Smythe Series (Crime)

Austerley & Kirkgordon Series (Fantasy)

1. Crescendo!
2. The Darkness at Dillingham
3. Dagon's Revenge
4. Ship of Doom

Supernatural and Elder Threat Assessment Agency (SETAA) Series (Fantasy)

1. Scarlett O'Meara: Beastmaster

Island Adventures Series (Cosy Fantasy Adventure)

1. Surface Tensions

Dark Wen Series (Horror Fantasy)

1. The Blasphemous Welcome
2. The Demon's Chalice

Chapter 01

S ister Priscilla knelt before the altar, bowed her head, and then crossed herself. She rose from her knees, bowing again to the figure hanging on the cross before her, turned, and walked along the cold stone floor. Her basic shoes clipped across the stone, resonating throughout the small chapel. It was only a short break that she was able to take, a short time to reflect and focus on her Lord before she'd have to make her way across town.

The bus went from the far end of the estate, and she had cut through, going by the river, taking off five minutes from the walk. It was frowned upon by the Mother Superior because she knew rightly that Priscilla did it to enjoy the wildflowers that were either side of the riverbank. She also enjoyed the flowing water, especially if it was rushing after a heavy rainfall.

As she reached the door of the chapel, she looked up at a grey sky that might be threatening rain and picked up her black raincoat, putting it on and zipping it up tight. She found a scarf for around her neck, again, one that wasn't approved of by Mother Superior, for it was so bright and jolly. It also had an Inverness Caledonian badge at the end of it.

'Football was a distraction from the real things in life,'

Mother Superior had said, in that rather dim and flat tone that she had. Sister Priscilla didn't dislike the Mother Superior, but she was a wise head on very old shoulders. She also hadn't moved with the times. The woman had spent a long time in a sheltered convent that didn't see much of the outside world.

Sister Priscilla, despite being almost fifty, had spent her time out in communities and never had such a solitary confinement. The Inverness order she was attached to was out in the community in so many ways. She always thought Mother Superior should lighten up a bit. After all, if you couldn't reach the people to be helped, what was the point? That was what they did, wasn't it? That was the job. Worship Him by helping them.

She took her handkerchief from the pocket of her coat and gave her nose a rub. Then, for a moment, she tried to hold the sneeze that was coming, failed miserably, and caught the blast within the handkerchief. She wiped her nose clean, replaced the handkerchief into the pocket and stepped out into what was a fresh breeze.

Someone was burning something not far away; she could smell it in the air. Not that she thought anything of it. There was a man nearby; he burned a lot of things for he seemed to have a lot of rubbish. It was all safe enough, but it made the air stink for a while.

Sister Priscilla started a brisk walk along the estate, almost racing the first five hundred metres before she could turn right onto a small path and find the riverbank. It had been raining yesterday—quite a downpour in the afternoon. She looked out to the water and saw it rushing over the small rocks. It was definitely not a stream, but more a small, winding river, something you could take a boat on. Possibly, you could take a canoe up it or a kayak or whatever they called them these days. Whatever they called them, the sound of rushing water hadn't changed, and created an ease in the soul.

There was a path along the side of the riverbank, and it bent with it; every one hundred metres or so, you were seeing a new vista, somewhere else that you couldn't have seen before, obscured by the hedge running alongside the path. The bends in the river at times were often severe.

Sister Priscilla found herself slowing down as she walked, breathing deeply, occasionally closing her eyes and letting the sound of the water just drift over her. As she turned around what must have been about the eighth or ninth corner, something caught her eye down by the riverbank. She walked over, bent down, and saw a flesh-coloured object in the water. Carefully, she reached down and on contact, realised it was flesh.

The overhanging bank had obscured most of whatever it was from her view, but undeterred, she knelt down, reaching around with both hands. Underneath the bank she could feel a shoulder and a head. *Holy Father, it was someone.*

Without hesitation, she reached down and tried to pull, but she couldn't find a way to move the body. Whoever this person was had been jammed in tightly. She stood up again and without bothering to lift her clothing, stepped into the water. It came up to her knee, soaking the bottom half of her attire, and she felt the cold of it, running through her ankles and feet. Enduring, she bent down, reached in underneath the bank, and almost toppled backwards when she saw a face looking back at her.

It could be no more than three or four years old. The eyes were wide open, staring out at nothing. *What do I do?* she

3

thought. *What do I do?* Somewhere in the back of her mind, she was trying to repress the scream, the yell, but suddenly it all flowed out. At the top of her voice, she let loose a cry that must have shaken the silence all along the riverbank. Yet, when she looked left and right, she saw no one.

Think, she said to herself, *Think.* As if on automatic, she blessed herself, her hand tracing a cross over her own body, before she reached in again with both hands and tried to pull the child out. She saw what the obstruction was, a rock placed across the legs. When she pulled it away at the second attempt, it allowed her to lift the small body out and place it up on the riverbank.

It was a boy, and she placed him face down while she tried to clamber out. She put her hand down beside him, pushing herself up onto the riverbank, and her eyes cast unwillingly towards his back. There were large cuts across it, many different symbols and strange marks.

Precise work, she thought and almost reviled herself for having that opinion. She went down to her knees again. At the side of the riverbank, she reached down grabbing the child and spinning him over. The marks were across the front of his torso as well. She looked at one in the centre of his body. It was a cross, but it was upside down. The other mark she didn't recognise. There were no other church-based symbols as far as she knew. Her eyes struggled to come away from the retched cross, the satanic symbol she knew, a twisting of her own precious Lord's sacrifice. *What to do?* she thought. *What to do?*

It was then she heard the pounding footsteps, and a man came running along the path. 'What?' he shouted. 'What?'

She looked up, total shock on his face as he looked at the

child beneath her.

'You need to call. You need to call. I have no phone on me. He needs help.'

'Is he alive?' said the man. He looked bizarre, stood in a pair of shorts and a running top, sweating, and yet his complexion was white, the colour having drained from it on seeing the child.

'I don't know,' said Priscilla. 'You need to go get help. Get an ambulance.'

Priscilla thought to herself, *What do I do now? What do I do? Dear God, help me. What do I do?* Something flowed from the recesses of her mind. *Of course, what had they said during the first aid course? She shouldn't assume the child was dead.*

She reached down, went to open the mouth, and placed her own lips on it to breathe air inside. *How did it go again? How did it go again?* She heard the man's footsteps running off and immersed herself in the techniques she learned in her first aid course, aware that if she didn't, she may just fall apart there and then.

* * *

How had this happened? How on earth was he caught up in this? Ryan McIntyre was a runner; he ran every day. He pounded down past the stream almost every day. Yet today, as he'd been running along, he'd heard a scream. A scream that had turned his blood cold. It wasn't a scream of shock or surprise; it was a scream of horror.

He had thought twice about whether or not he should run to it. Now that he had, now that he'd seen the nun on the ground kneeling over that body, he knew he shouldn't have. He knew he should have turned and run the other way, continued on his remaining five miles. When she'd screamed at him about getting help, he should have taken his phone out. He should have simply picked up the phone, dialled 999, and spoken to the operator. He should have asked for an ambulance, asked for the police, asked for whoever, got help, and then gone and stood beside the nun, to see what he could have done for her.

The trouble was when he saw that little figure, everything began to shut down. Every sinew in him screamed, 'Get away.' *What were all the marks on the front of the child? What was that?* She'd said, 'Help,' and he'd turned and ran around the corner. Now taking his phone from where it was zipped away inside his running shorts, he dialled the three numbers for help.

'Which service do you require?'

'Ambulance, police. No, amb-—one of them.'

'One moment. Just connecting you.'

The moment seemed to go on forever. Ryan turned and looked at the corner he'd run from. Through the hedge, he could see the nun was still there. She was still with the child.

'Ambulance service. What's the problem?'

'The child—he's covered in cuts and wounds. He's been in the river. I think it's . . . well, I think he's been in the river. I . . . I . . .'

'Calm down, sir. Calm down. Just tell me what's happened. Slowly.'

'I heard a scream. I heard a scream. I came around the corner. There's a nun there. She's over the body of a small child. I don't know if he's alive or not. She told me to get help. The child has cuts, deep marks, markings. I . . . I don't know.'

'You require an ambulance, sir?'

'Yes, yes. We need an ambulance.'

'Where are you?'

'I'm at the riverbank. The riverbank in Inverness. The—oh, hell, what is it? It's the . . .'

It dawned on him that if he simply put on his app for running, it would give the grid reference.

'Can you take a grid reference, a post code? The phone says it's . . .' He passed over the postcode.

'Just a moment,' said the voice on the other end of the line. 'We've got the river. You're on the path by the river, sir. Is that correct?'

'Yes, that's correct.' Ryan's head was spinning, and his eyes were looking at the other side of the stream, casting looks up and down and around as he twisted and turned, speaking quickly, unable to stand still. Then his eyes looked down. There was something down by the bank. It looked rather strange because it was obscured.

'There's somebody else there,' he said, randomly into the phone.

'I'm sorry, sir?'

'I think there's . . . there's . . .' He put the phone down and against all reason for his own preservation, he ran and jumped into the stream. He ignored the cold that flooded across his legs as he fought across it, reaching the far bank. Several bags had drifted and other rubbish had also collected in the eddy by the bank, but he'd seen something flesh-coloured there and it had reminded him so starkly of the child on the bank.

He pulled away some of the rubbish and saw a face looking back at him. It had blonde hair, a woman's face. He pulled at her, trying to get her out from the small cut-in stream she'd gone into. As he did so, he realised her hands were behind her back and as she twisted, he could see where they were tied.

7

She's like a dead weight, he thought, then almost cursed himself for thinking the phrase. He dragged her, pulled her up onto the bank, but it was awkward because her hands were behind her and she offered no assistance. He began to slap her face.

'Are you there? Are you there?' he shouted. 'Come on. Bloody hell, come on.' The woman was fully clothed, wearing a skirt, a blouse, and a coat which had weighed her down, making it so difficult to pull her out. Just above the noise of the river, he could hear someone shouting through his phone. He realised he had left the call handler waiting.

What should I do? CPR. I don't know how to do CPR. I've never done CPR. God, I never thought I'd need it. Should I run and get the nun to work on her? Should I go back to the phone? I'd better go and get the phone. I need the phone because if I'm not there, they might think it's a prank.

He jumped back into the water. He didn't know if he could get any paler for his blood ran cold, and as he picked up the phone, he struggled to say what he wanted to.

'Another body. Another. There's a woman dead. Another . . .'

'We're on our way. We're on our way, sir. Just keep talking to me. Keep talking to me; tell me what's going on.'

Ryan jabbered on and on, but he stood looking at the woman across from him and all he thought was he should have turned back. When he heard the scream, he should have run as fast as he could in the opposite direction.

Chapter 02

'Mr Macleod, so you would say that Mr Ross here is a fine example of a man?'

'It's Detective Inspector Macleod, and yes, I would. Ross is one of our best. He's a thoroughly decent human being. He thought a lot about this, thought a lot about how work would fit in with trying to raise a child.'

'You don't see an issue with the . . . it being two men bringing up the child?'

Macleod sunk back in the seat in Ross's front living room. He could see across from him the younger woman was eagerly awaiting his answer. The easy thing for Macleod to do was to turn around and say, 'Absolutely not. I'm totally with it. I've shrugged off any prejudice from the past. I have absolutely no worries or fears about the child being brought up by two men. I think it's exactly the same as having a man and a woman raise a child.'

However, that wasn't what Macleod thought. He wasn't against Ross bringing up a child with his partner Angus. He just struggled to see how it worked. When a child got influence from two sides, it would seem better with a caring, nurturing mother and a strong father. Or was that not just stereotypical nonsense. Macleod realised that he had no frame of reference here, apart from his own mother and father.

They'd been very traditional back in Lewis. Father had been the head of the house, but in truth, his mother had been quiet, yet the one that kept everything going. His father had not been particularly nice to her at times, telling her to be quiet. Macleod wasn't sure that it was the healthiest of relationships they'd had. His own relationship had never culminated in a child, and certainly his current one with Jane wasn't going to. They were well beyond that age. Why on earth was this woman asking him his opinion? Ross was a decent a bloke as he knew, but he couldn't lie. He shouldn't lie.

'I've got to be honest,' said Macleod. 'I have no idea if two men or two women bringing up a child will mess them up any more than a man and a woman can do together. I don't know why you're asking me that. What I can tell you is he's a thoroughly decent man and he'll do everything for that child. He'll try and raise that child as best as he can, as I believe so will Angus.'

'And yet you call him Ross,' said the woman. 'It's very formal, isn't it?'

'It's what he wants to be called. He's always been Ross. I wouldn't call him anything else. He still calls me sir. We ditched that a while back, but Ross is the only one who still does it.'

'It's just a respect I have for him,' Ross interjected, and got a frown from the woman. She had large spectacles, yet she was able to bring them to the end of her nose and look over the top at him when she wanted to. Macleod hoped he wasn't screwing up this interview process.

Of all the people he worked with, Ross had brought him

in, maybe hoping that the gravitas of a detective inspector would work. Well, she'd called him a mister for a start so that obviously wasn't on her mind.

'Can I ask you something about this work?' said the woman. 'How do you find the time schedule? What are the hours that you work?'

'Well, I have to be honest,' said Macleod, 'At times it can be quite a strain, but how it relates to a child, I don't know. I don't have any.'

'Not found the time for them?' asked the woman.

'My wife died,' Macleod said bluntly. 'My wife committed suicide on the Isle of Lewis. I fled to Glasgow, hid myself in cases down there until I found a delightful woman just before I moved back up to Inverness. Didn't find the time doesn't really fit.'

He cast a glance at Ross, worried that he'd overstepped the mark, but he saw Ross almost laugh. Macleod came across as if he'd been hurt by the comment, but Ross knew better. This was Macleod at his best. It was the same way he'd take a suspect, focus in on them, crushing them beneath his comment but the woman didn't seem to be reacting that way.

'There was a fair degree of instability in your work life. Can we expect that in Ross's, too?'

'All life's unstable,' said Macleod. 'I mean seriously, all life is unstable. When have you ever known a home that isn't?'

The woman gave a deep cough and Macleod felt his phone vibrate in his pocket. 'Excuse me,' he said, 'I need to look at this.' There was a text message from Hope, simply saying there'd been a murder down by the riverbank on the east side of Inverness and his presence was required.

'I'm afraid this interview's going to have to be cut,' said

11

Macleod. 'I've got to go.'

'This is rather important,' said the woman. 'We need to ascertain if Mr Ross is fit, if Alan and Angus are ideal parents for whatever child we place with them.'

'Ross and Angus are fit. I've got a dead body to go to,' said Macleod snappily. 'There isn't a fitter man you could give a child to. Now if you could excuse me, someone needs my help.'

'Do you need me?' asked Ross.

'Finish up here, then come down straight after, please,' said Macleod. Then he turned back to the woman. 'Whatever else you've got to do, don't delay with it. I need my detective with me. The early time during an investigation is when we need to start moving quickly and Ross is a big part of my team. Delighted to meet you.'

With that, Macleod turned, grabbed his coat off the seat, and marched out through the living room door. He heard Ross get up and simply shouted back over his shoulder that he was fine, and Ross should follow as soon as. As soon as he'd stepped out of the house, Macleod picked up the phone and dialled Hope's number.

'What's happened?' he asked.

'Need to get down quickly to this one, Seoras. We've got a child found at the riverbank by a nun. Child has markings on it. Symbols carved into the front and back of the torso.'

'What?' said Macleod. 'Symbols?'

'That's correct. I haven't let anybody else know other than those of us down here.'

'Well, get a large cordon in effect. That area needs sealed off. That's not information we want going out.'

'Of course,' said Hope. 'Pulling as much uniform as I can to assist us.'

'Good,' said Macleod, calming down somewhat. 'You said symbols?'

'Yes, symbols. No idea what symbols except for one.'

'What's that?'

'It's an upside-down cross smack in the middle of the front of the child's torso. I think it's affected the nun somewhat, but I'm only just here. I haven't spoken to her properly yet.'

'Just make sure she's looked after,' said Macleod. He could feel the hollow in his own stomach. An upside-down cross. He'd gone through quite a change in his own beliefs from the strictness of a Lewis upbringing. Reared in a free church where you sat and you listened to the sermon. You didn't speak, towed the line. Nowadays he still believed—very firmly believed in a God and the saviour that was up on the cross—but he did it with a joy he thought; it felt less of an obligation and more of a willingness. Jane had helped in that, but he could understand how the nun would be more than spooked.

Macleod found his car, started the engine, and drove out into the Inverness traffic. As he drove, he got a phone call and pulled his phone out, placing it on the seat beside him. It was Hope again. He thought about clicking the hands-free button that would connect the phone to the car and he'd be able to simply speak out loud as he drove. But in all honesty, he wasn't sure he would press the right button. He was clueless when it came to some of this stuff. Macleod pulled over, switched off the engine, and answered the call from Hope.

'I wasn't finished,' she said.

'There's more?' said Macleod. 'How worse can it get?'

'Well, it appears that the nun found the boy. She screamed for help. A jogger turned up and while he was on the phone to the ambulance, he found a female body in the water and pulled her out.'

'You're going to tell me she's covered in symbols as well, are you?' said Macleod.

'No,' said Hope, 'not at all. She's dead though. She was in the water, hands tied behind her back. She's fully dressed. Skirt, blouse, jacket from what we can tell. We've obviously not gone too close. Waiting for Jona to deal with the forensic side.'

'Of course,' said Macleod. 'Good. Is anybody there for your witnesses?'

'Two of them are in the back of an ambulance at the moment, being dealt with. Both in heavy shock. I've asked them not to leave for the hospital if they need to go until I okay it. Unless something was obviously direly wrong with them.'

'Good,' said Macleod. 'Is the DCI aware?'

'Not yet. I haven't phoned him.'

'Do that,' said Macleod. 'It's the symbology and stuff, just in case it gets out to the press. I want him to be ready in case he gets asked questions.'

'How is the new one?' she asked. 'It feels like we're on a spinning top at the moment. New one coming along every few months.'

'They reckon this one's going to be here long-term, but if I'm truthful, I've only met him a few times. Gave me all the standard bumph that you do. I did check out where he'd been before, down in the Edinburgh area. They seemed quite happy with him but it's a promotion up. I don't want him getting blindsided by this.'

'I'm on it,' said Hope.

'Where's Clarissa?'

'On her way,' said Hope. 'I was in the office and nearest. Clarissa was out, just tying up some odd ends from previous investigations. To be honest, you'll probably get here before her.'

'Good. We're all set. Everything's going in motion.'

'It is. How did it go with Ross?'

'I have no idea. I don't think she was impressed that I was a detective. I don't think she was impressed that we worked long hours. I don't think she's impressed at all. Then she asked me if I thought two men would be ideal for bringing up a child. How do I know, Hope?'

'You didn't turn around and say that God made man and woman, did you?'

He went to react, to bite, but then he stopped. 'No, I didn't and that's a very dated remark you're making.'

'Sorry,' she said. 'Just trying to break away from the mood down here. It's not pleasant.'

'How long has it been since we had a kid die?' asked Macleod.

'I'm not sure I've had one with you. I've seen it before when I worked in Glasgow. Not sure we worked one up here.'

'No,' said Macleod. 'I'm not sure either. Keep an eye on the team, everyone from the basic constable right up to the top. It's different with children. You know that.'

'I do. I know it's different. See you shortly.'

'One more thing, Hope,' he said. Then there was a knock at the windscreen. He looked up and saw a traffic warden pointing down at the yellow lines that Macleod was parked on.

'It'll wait,' he said. 'See you there.'

Macleod pressed the electric window on the passenger side, which allowed the traffic warden to pop her head inside the car.

'Detective Inspector Macleod, just pulled over to make a call, urgent with regard to a case.'

'There was room further up,' she said. 'Doesn't give you a right to just pull in and sit on the yellow lines.'

'I said Detective Inspector Macleod working a case. Important phone call. Needed to take it safely.'

'Like I said, double yellow lines. I'll let this go, inspector. But next time.'

Macleod could feel himself seething. He wanted to scream at her, 'I've got a dead child I'm going to. He's got symbols carved on his body. I don't know what on earth's gone on down there, but his mum or some other woman is dead too.' But instead, Macleod simply nodded and pressed the button for the electric window to rise while the warden still had her elbows on it. She jumped back somewhat. He let the window rise right to the top, started the engine, and as he pulled away, he gave a little wave out the window. *Yes, I'll just find a proper parking spot,* he thought, as he pulled back out into the melee of the Inverness traffic.

Chapter 03

Macleod pulled up in a car park that was located just off the river and where the police cordon was being maintained. In stepping out of his car, he received a nod and an 'Inspector,' from one of the uniform constables before he strode through to the path beyond.

'It's just on the left, sir,' came the shout from over his shoulder. Macleod followed the instruction, making his way over three hundred metres down to a bend in the path where he saw numerous lights. Dark had fallen, and lights had been set up to illuminate the scene, where Jona Nakamura and her forensic team would work.

As he approached, he could see Hope McGrath, his sergeant, issuing instructions and dressed in a white crime scene overall. In one hand was another one, and it was because she anticipated his arrival.

'Hope, how are we doing?'

'Not much difference since you got off the phone with me. I had a word with the DCI. I expect he'll be phoning you, probably in about twenty minutes, expecting you to have some sort of solution.'

'That's unfair. He may have to wait twenty-five,' said

Macleod. He tried to give a wry smile, but the two of them looked at each other with serious eyes. 'How old is the kid?' asked Macleod.

'We think four. Jona says it's not pretty.'

'Didn't think it would be,' said Macleod. 'Give me the outfit and we'll get cracking.'

Macleod took the overall that she handed to him, stepped to one side of the path, and put it on before taking some covers for his shoes as well. He zipped the hood up over his head and the pair of them, dressed in white, made their way to Jona.

The diminutive Japanese woman was kneeling over the body of a young child. The body was naked, extremely pale, but Macleod thought at least he looked at rest. As he got closer, he was able to see the cuts that decorated the child's front, including the upside-down cross, which from his position was currently sitting in its correct attitude.

'Detective Inspector. It's not pretty, to say the least,' said Jona.

'Let's just run it by the book,' replied Macleod. 'I think we'll all be emotional about it, but let's just keep it professional.'

'Of course. The child was murdered before the marks on his body were inflicted. He was killed by a stab to the heart from behind, causing a massive failure. If it's any comfort, he probably would've gone quite quickly. Afterward, he was mutilated but in a very precise way. These cuts take time. Looking at them, I'd have said probably at least half an hour to do them with this precision.'

'Very steady hands,' said Hope. 'A butcher?'

'With all due respect to our butchers,' said Macleod, 'they take a big knife and whack through beef or pig. They don't sit putting delicate patterns on it. Even when they score a pork

18

belly, it's not like this. No, this is more like a surgeon with the precision that's going on there.'

'I think some of our surgeons would be quite pleased with the level of detail,' said, Jona, 'if not why it was done. I'll try and see if I can find what sort of knife would do this. It's usually a specialist blade. Regarding the markings, at the moment I'm unclear what they are. Obviously, the upside-down cross is of a satanic nature, but in truth used by so many groups, it's going to be hard to pin that one down. The other symbols I don't recognise at all, even with my Asian heritage.'

'I take it we've got photographs of them.'

'Front and back,' said Jona. She turned and waved to a colleague of hers who brought up an envelope, which she handed to Macleod. He took out the photographs, identified the ones that were on the front and then started peering at the others.

'Where was the second body?' asked Macleod.

'The child's mother,' said Jona. 'Well, kind of identified as his mother. It's further down. I should say we believe it's the mother. We've had someone come looking for them. The pair of them. If Ross was here, we could get him to chase that up.'

'Ross is on his way. He was at a rather important meeting.'

'Yes, I heard,' said Jona. 'Probably not a great thing to come out to after that.'

'Not a great thing for any of us to come to,' said Macleod. 'Go on, about the mother.'

'She may have been dumped up here. She wasn't killed like the child. She was tied up, arms behind her, put into the river at some point. She's a bit further downstream, but she seems to have got caught in some sort of eddy or, however it's happened, the river's held her in underneath the bank. I don't know if

19

the killer wanted us to find her further downstream or if they wanted her to be picked up first and then a search, meaning the child was found. It's hard to tell . . . rather strange thing to just dump them in a river like this.'

'You said she wasn't killed here,' said Macleod.

'Oh, she died here,' said Jona. 'She died of drowning. She was put into the water, but I'm not sure if it was the intention to drown her or simply to have her scared and floating downstream to be found alive. She would then shout and yell for help and eventually she'd come and find the child. It's all very much supposition for now. All I can tell you is that drowning was the cause of death. There's not another mark on her from what I can tell. Nothing sexual, nothing indicating violence other than bound hands. I'll do a full toxicology of her blood, but my suspicion is she was drugged in some way. Incapacitated, tied up, and dumped.'

Macleod stared up and down the river, which was rapidly losing the light. The bright lights where they stood illuminated the scene, but beyond it, everything was getting dim at the night's arrival.

Macleod heard some commotion further up the path and a voice he recognised asking where she should go. Clarissa was on the way.

'Sergeant,' shouted Macleod up the riverbank, 'get a suit on and join us.' He saw her wave her hand at him, parading down the riverbank in her trademark shawl, and he turned back to Jona with a sombre look.

'Symbology is never good, is it? Serial killers, symbology often comes into it. We need to track down where these are coming from, what they're about.'

'I'd have to agree with you there, Inspector,' said Jona.

'Where was the mother found exactly?' he asked.

Jona stood up, walked down the riverbank, and then pointed across it to where the mother lay after being left there by the jogger.

'The man that found her,' said Jona, 'he's in a bad way. He's being looked after by paramedics, but I'm not sure how much you'll get out of him. It's quite shaken him. The nun who found the child though, she was much more with it. Even so, to be honest, I don't think you'll learn a lot from them. I believe the constables have been taking basic statements about where they found the child, and where they found the mother just so we can put everything together, but I think that's all they have done as far as I can tell.'

Hope nodded in agreement.

'Well, we'll chase it up anyway. Got to be a shock for them.' Macleod turned and looked back up the riverbank where he could see the lights but couldn't see Clarissa because of the bend in the path.

He heard a shout and turned and strode with Hope back up to the first body. He saw Clarissa at a distance, now garbed in a white overall, hood up over her hair, looking at him in a dour fashion.

'Now, I warn you, it's not pretty, said Macleod, and Clarissa nodded, walking forward rather sheepishly. 'Jona will take you through it again. I just need to go and have a think.'

He stepped away, allowing room for Clarissa to walk forward and examine the body, and stood under one of the large lights. It was about two seconds later when he heard the first gulp, and then the second, and then Clarissa raced past him, emptying the contents of her stomach into the hedge beyond. She snorted as she bent over, then lifted herself back up.

21

'Jesus,' she said. 'Jesus.' Her face twisted, looked at Macleod, and suddenly he knew she was ready for a rebuke. He didn't care for the Lord's name to be taken in vain, but the woman had just gone pale. He'd forgotten she'd been an art detective, chasing down pieces of work that had been stolen, shenanigans in the market. Since she'd come to the team, she sometimes found the crime scenes difficult. This was different though.

'The first time you've seen a child like this?' He asked.

She stared at him, eyes narrowing. 'When have you ever seen a child like this? He's got cuts and marks, and . . .' She stepped forward again. Whatever else was still inside her stomach was ejected rapidly. When she stood back up, Macleod handed her a handkerchief.

'It's okay,' he said. 'It's okay. You won't be the first.'

A voice came from over his shoulder. 'She's not the first today,' said Jona. 'One of mine. Yes, well.'

Macleod put his arm around Clarissa as she was bent over, looked at her face and tried to ignore the globules that were falling off her mouth. 'It's not normal,' he said. 'You should be reviled. In time you'll learn to hold your stomach, but there's no nice about this.'

She sniffed, wiped her nose and the liquid that was coming off the bottom of her chin, and in Clarissa fashion, she stood up, turned and marched back to the body. 'Talk to me, Jona,' she said. 'Talk to me quickly.'

Macleod stepped away, followed by Hope, and he turned to his sergeant, whispering in her ear. 'Just keep a good eye on her.'

'On all of them, Seoras. I keep an eye on all of them.' With that, they looked up to see Ross arriving. Macleod had been at his house earlier where he had looked nervous but happy with the process that was about to go on. Now his face was grim, something that was fairly unusual on Ross's face. He took everything in his stride. Everything.

'Everything go okay back there?' asked Macleod.

'We'll see,' said Ross. 'I'm not convinced. Neither is Angus, but who knows? Just who knows? What about here? How are we?'

'Cordon in place,' said Hope. 'We've got two witnesses sitting in ambulances. We need to go through thoroughly what they saw. We've gone through an initial statement just in case they lost any information before we spoke to them properly. We're keeping a wide cordon. Everyone away from here.'

'What's happened?'

'Oh, I thought Seoras told you.'

'The Inspector left before in a rush, so we didn't have time to talk.'

'Suit on,' said Macleod. 'Suit on. We'll take you to see the body. A young child, about four years old, killed by stabbing to the heart and then has symbols carved into the body. It's not pretty. The mother is further downstream. She was alive when they dumped her with hands tied behind her back into the water. She may have been unconscious from something else. However, she drowned in the river, found by a jogger who showed up. The kid was found by a nun. As Hope said, they're both in the ambulances.'

'What do you want me to do?' he asked.

'Give us a second. We'll pull Clarissa over as well.' It took a moment before Clarissa came back and Macleod could see the tears welling up, but she was determined and although she sniffed a few times, she was ready.

'This is how we play it,' said Macleod. 'Hope, you have the

initial scene with Ross. Get all the interviews done. Make sure nobody gets inside here. Give Jona every help she needs to get this place gone over with a fine-tooth comb. Check out our nun. Why was she here? What was she doing? Check our jogger. Why is he on this route? What happened? Confirm the identity of mother and child. Clarissa, the symbols. You start on that. You're used to the art world. You are used to unusual things. Do you recognise any of them?'

'Some look South American,' said Clarissa. 'I can't identify any of them. Just the feel of them. Obviously, the one in the middle, everyone knows, but strange for Satanists. Don't they sacrifice rather than just dump? Doesn't seem credible.'

Macleod could see she was struggling to get the words out, but she was doing what they needed to do. Push away the revulsion, push back everything that was stopping you from doing your job, and get the job done.

'Well, you've got to find someone who can get these symbols identified. I'm worried that this is a serial killer. Unusual to do something like that on the skin if you don't intend to repeat it. Why? Was it some sort of a cult thing for a blessing? Is it some type of ritual killing? Did the mother do something wrong? Did the child? Although I don't know what a four-year-old child can do wrong to deserve this. Let's get on it.

'Hope, Ross, check through our victims. Check through our witnesses. Look for CCTV as well, although I can't see any here, but the street outside. Get a canvas going. Sweep the area. Get uniform to go door to door. Get them to stop cars. I'm going to talk to the DCI because this is going to have major repercussions in the press. We're going to need to do a statement about what's happened. I think we'll keep the symbology out of the way for the minute; that's not something they need to know. Also, in case anyone else mentions it, it's better it's not in the public eye. We'll know they got it from somewhere else.'

'Well, you heard him,' said Hope. 'Let's go to it.' Hope and Ross marched off together, discussing how they would tackle the two witnesses. Macleod looked over at Clarissa, who smiled at him, but it was short-lived before the horror on her face came back.

'I know, I know but we signed up for this, and we need to function. Try and channel it. Try and channel the anger. Put it into what you do and get me an understanding of what these symbols are.'

Clarissa nodded and then left the inspector alone on the path. He pulled out his phone, ready to contact the DCI. Today was the day he was glad he'd never had children because he wasn't sure if he had, what looking at the scene just behind him would've done to him.

Chapter 04

Macleod was feeling sick as he approached the press conference. There was never a time that he enjoyed dealing with the press. Indeed, on many occasions, he'd simply handed it off to Hope to do because she was much more engaging, capable of handling them better than he. It wasn't a case that they could trap him. He just seethed with anger underneath, seeing them as vultures getting in the way of running a case.

He'd have to sit up with the DCI on this one as well and possibly on future ones; even the assistant chief constable might come along as well. The public's interest was sure to be piqued by what they discovered, but for now it would be kept simple. A child had died; the mother was dead too. Inquiries were ongoing. He wondered if anyone would ask about how the child died. Again, inquiries were ongoing. There was no need for things like that to be brought out at this time. No need to put out to the public what he preferred to keep under wraps so he could see what people knew without hearing it from the press, or reading their stories. Some people gave themselves away like that. He knew in police work, you needed all the breaks you could get.

His phone rang and he looked down, ready to kill the call, but saw it was his partner Jane. He pressed the answer button, placing the phone up to his ear.

'I heard it on the news. I take it you're investigating,' she said.

'I am. Sorry. Haven't had a chance to call you yet.'

'It's all right. I know the score. Ross is usually the first one to call me anyway. You were down at his, weren't you?'

'Yes,' said Macleod. 'I was doing that supporting character witness interview for him, but then this kicked off.'

There was a silence on the phone.

'Are you okay?' asked Jane.

'It's a child. Child and mother and it's not very good.'

'Okay,' said Jane. 'If you need me to bring anything down to you, it's not a problem.'

'Thanks. You're always there. Might need you to have a talk to Clarissa at some point.'

'Did she . . . ?'

'Oh, she reacted when she saw it. Sometimes it's good to talk to somebody off the force who understands.'

'Well, I don't understand. I just know how to help you guys.'

'Well, that's what I meant. Look, sorry, love, I'm going to have to go. Just about to go into a press conference. I can see the DCI coming, so that means it's imminent.'

'Okay. Take care, love. Seoras, remember, I love you.'

'I know,' he said. 'I know.' Macleod closed the call, and then greeted the DCI as he approached him.

'You're on top of things, then.' The new DCI was called Lawson. Quite appropriate for a policeman, and no doubt he'd been the butt of jokes through the years. He was a short, stocky man with a firm handshake that Macleod thought nearly broke

27

his hand, but he seemed competent, both from his record and the initial times they'd seen each other.

'Yes. We're on top of it, having spoken to the witnesses. Once this is done, I'm going back for a meeting with the team. We'll kick off on the investigation lines. Two possible lines at the moment, sir. I'm thinking there's this symbology that was on the child and there's also the mother and child and their basic life—we can have a look around that. See who's involved with them. We're doing the obvious sweeps, CCTV and that, but it's early to have got anything from it, and so far, we haven't. It's a good place to commit a murder, or at least to dump the body, because there's no CCTV. It's fairly quiet and remote and where they had stashed the child's body would have been hidden away from casual people passing on the river. It's possible they may have wanted the mother to be a calling card. We have a theory that she got dumped in the river and was meant to float downstream, but she got trapped.'

'Calling card, why?' asked the DCI.

'As I said, it's just a thought,' said Macleod. 'The symbology, that's one of the best ways to go.'

'Who've you got chasing that up?'

'Urquhart, Sergeant Urquhart.'

'Clarissa Urquhart. Yes, she came across from the art side. Antiquities and things. How is she doing?'

'She's all right. She's old school, knows the score. Can handle herself,' said Macleod.

'You think she's the woman for this symbology?'

'She's seen more symbols than I ever have,' said Macleod. 'Oh, she'll go and get experts in and that, but she knows how to talk to them. Clarissa can work with the intelligent as much as kick the arse of the lowly.'

The DCI seemed taken aback for a moment. 'Interesting way to put it, Inspector. Anyway, let's get this done. I'll take the bulk of the questions. Usual line at the moment. Given what's happened, we don't want to panic the public, so I'm totally with going right down the line. Bodies found, investigation continuing. We don't mention the symbology.'

'Agreed.' Macleod held his hand forward for the DCI to walk on through the door that led out to the hall beyond where the press was gathered.

* * *

Macleod parked in the car park he'd been at earlier and the same constable nodded him through the police line. He made his way to the mobile unit set up at the other end of the car park, far back from the cordon, where he would be joining his team for a brief meeting. He knew he'd be the first there but was surprised when he opened the door to find several flasks sitting on the side of the small meeting room. He opened one up and smelled coffee. It was his brand, the one he enjoyed. Every time, Ross never ceased to amaze him. He poured a cup, took out his phone and sent a text message to his group advising he was ready for the meeting as soon as they were. It was only a minute later when Ross walked through the room.

'Coffee all right for you, sir?' he said.

'How do you do that?'

'Well, you need your coffee. You always need your coffee,' said Ross. 'I thought you'd probably need it a lot more today. We need to keep things as normal as possible, so we don't get spooked. We keep ourselves focused.'

'Did I tell you that?' said Macleod.

'No, sir. Sergeant McGrath told us that.'

A few minutes later, the rest of his core team had arrived, Jona the last in, still dressed in her forensic outfit. She sat down at the far end of the table, but Macleod stood and poured her the coffee and brought it to her.

'First off,' he said as he placed it in front of Jona. 'Everybody okay? If you're not, say now.'

He spun round, looked over towards Clarissa, who gave a grim nod back. 'Okay. Ross advises me that we keep everything as normal, so get the coffees out and let's get talking. What have we got, Ross?'

As Macleod sat down, Ross stood up at the table and placed a photograph on it.

'The woman we found dead today is Amanda Hughes. She's thirty-six, a single mother living on the nearby council estate, the Rathgordon Estate, and the child with her is her son Steven. There's a buggy nearby, which currently, Jona's team are looking at, but how it got there, we are unsure. We have an address for the woman, but we do know that she was seen in the supermarket this morning with Steven in that buggy from CCTV footage offered by the store. It appears that the store detective recognised her. They traced it through on the CCTV and she was there. That would've been early, though, possibly around eight o'clock this morning.'

'Any idea when she died?' asked Macleod.

'She died not long before she was found. I would place it maybe an hour or two at the most. The child, however, died several hours before that. That's a best guess,' said Jona. 'I'm going to get that more accurate for you, but that's what we're looking at.'

'How much blood would have come from those cuts?' asked

Macleod.

'Well, that's something else,' said Jona. 'I said originally the child was stabbed in the heart, thereby killing the child, and then worked on for the symbols. Having had a closer look, and I'll confirm this when we get back to the lab, but I think the knife was actually inserted in a way to cut the heart. In effect, there's a symbol of sorts on it.'

Clarissa took a big deep breath and Macleod heard her say, 'Jesus,' again. He didn't look over at her, merely ignored it, and looked back to Jona. 'When that happened,' he said, 'I take it that would've caused quite a lot of blood.'

'Absolutely, but there's no clothes with the child. The mother probably wasn't stripped or else she would have had to have been redressed, which seems unlikely. My belief is still that she was knocked out in some fashion, possibly drugged.'

'Any luck with CCTV around here?' asked Macleod.

Ross shook his head. 'Nothing so far. I've got some from the estate. We've got other car parks, et cetera. But it's a lot of material to go through, sir. It's going to take time. I'm setting up a team to look through it currently. I won't get near it myself; I've got other things to do here.'

Macleod nodded. That was normal. Likelihood of finding something on the CCTV was unlikely and there were plenty of other people who could look for a face.

'Don't forget to go through her bank details. See if there's any extortion involved. We'll need to see if she's involved in any groups.'

'I'm going out there after this meeting to see her house, meet the neighbours, find out what sort of life she had,' said Hope.

'Good,' said Macleod.

'And I'm off to see the symbology professor up at the

university,' said Clarissa.

'That's all good. What made her special?' said Macleod. 'That's the question. Was she? The child is four, and a small child. The symbols are on the child. Is the mother just an expendable casualty? Is the real thing about the child here? If so, are we talking something sacrificial? Are we talking rites or are we just talking a lunatic?'

'It's not some wild lunatic,' said Jona, very matter of fact. 'To carve like that into the flesh, you have to . . .' Jona stopped, looked over at Clarissa, whose hand had gone up to her mouth. She put her hand up for a moment, bent over slightly, then she reached up for her coffee cup, took a large sip, and drank it down.

'Go on,' she said. 'Go on.'

'You'd have to be of a very trained hand, very steady, neat work. We could be looking at some sort of craftsman or woman, someone who's used to doing articulation.'

'Good point, Jona,' said Macleod. 'What else, though?'

'Physically strong. Had to subdue the mother, had to bring her here. There's the buggy up close, but there's no method of dragging the mother here and the child.'

'How close could they get, Ross?' asked Macleod. 'Where's the nearest car park?'

'You'd have to drag the body at least three hundred metres. The mother over his shoulder? He'd have to be an absolute brute.'

'Or there's more than one,' said Hope. 'Could be looking at a team. If the symbology's right and it's some sort of cult, that would fit.'

'How many cults do we have around here?' asked Macleod. 'I don't seem to be aware of them.'

'Isn't that the point of a cult?' said Clarissa. 'These organisations, societies, they do exist now. Most of them are, I guess, a bit like the Masons. A lot of people think they do good within the community. Some people are against them, like the Presbyterian churches. Others don't see them as anything but a boys' club of sorts. However, this is another level to actively kill as a cult. You would certainly be much more underground.'

'Dark web,' said Ross. 'I've got people looking into that, trying to see if there's any conversations highlighting what's happened.'

'Good,' said Macleod. 'Just be aware we're going to be under pressure with this one. It's a child; that always leads to "find the killer more quickly." We don't; we find the killer the same way as we've always found the killer. We go through our methods, and we stick with them. Don't become distracted. If anybody's asking for information, it's the usual "inquiries are continuing." Nothing more, nothing less. It's very easy to cause a panic, especially amongst parents. At the moment, we keep on with the two-track idea, Clarissa off to chase up the symbols, Hope looking after the woman's life and the child, where they came from, what they did. Ross, running things here. I'll keep the overview. I'll drop in with you when I deem it necessary and I'll also be the front liaison up top with the DCI to the press.'

'You okay to do that?' asked Hope, and Macleod turned around, giving her an almost-annoyed look.

'I can handle the press. I just don't like to, but you need to be free to run and investigate on this. Besides, you'd be too much more engaging with them. I can sit and do the belligerent look.'

'You can that,' said Clarissa.

'Good, so we all know what we've got to do. Get back out

there; get on with it. Jona, any more help, let us know. Oh, Clarissa, when you're done, give us a shout. We'll come back, we'll reconvene, and we'll work out where we're going again, but I want a picture built up. I want a picture built up with our murderer from the symbols. I want a picture built up of the woman and her child. We do it quickly, so we can see who might be involved, because you don't know if another one's round the corner.'

Macleod gave a stare across the table. He wasn't obliged to, but he felt he had to. The situation was grim, a dark matter before them. He stood and watched his team leave the room, first Jona, who seemed detached as ever, followed by Ross, brisk in his movement. Following them was Clarissa, and he swore her eyes still held tears within them. Once she'd closed the door, Hope stood up from the table, making her way to him.

'She's going to struggle.'

'Yes, we're all going to struggle, but she's going to struggle in particular,' said Macleod. 'That's why she's on the symbology. Get her back to the world she knows. Get her back to doing what she does best. Same with you. Go on. Go find me out what's up with this woman. Find me out why they were targets.'

Macleod watched his redheaded sergeant disappear, then sat down with the flask of coffee in front of him. He poured himself another cup and picked up his phone. He reported back to the DCI what had been said in the brief meeting. Not because there was anything ground shaking, but because it was best to keep in touch. With this DCI being so new, he wanted to make sure that the conversation went both ways.

Upside-down cross, he thought. *Satanic elements, cults*. There was a chill that came across Macleod, not one that he could rationalise, but one that was definitely there. He hoped this was a one-off, hoped that this murderer was some freak madman and not some cult grouping. The trouble was he didn't believe it.

Chapter 05

Hope entered the Rathgordon Estate, one which she had not been in many times before. She'd obviously heard of it, and it was far from the worst estate that Inverness had. In truth, most estates in Inverness were more than reasonable. Yes, they'd had that friction more recently but that had been whipped up deliberately. The team had successfully managed to locate the cause of it and now she looked around the great buildings with flat after flat.

She recognised a similar trait here. Sure, there was disaffection, the large number of youths running around, or else hanging on street corners as they got slightly older. She could see some of the residents watching them but also an old lady walking past them, unfettered by them, just going about her daily business.

The day itself was reasonably bright but the morning had cast a red shadow, and Hope wondered if the rain was coming later on. She looked down at the phone, checking the maps function, and made a left and a right before pulling up in front of what looked like a semi-detached house. It had that typical Scottish trait, where the house, which previously may have been semi-detached, now had four flats within it.

Then she checked the number against the address she had been given. Stepping out of the car, Hope was nearly taken out by a kid all dressed in black on a bike. She watched him stare at her, the bike continuing to race on until he almost crashed into a parked car. His head whipped around just in time, he braked, almost fell off the bike and then looked back at her, embarrassed. He was probably late teens, and he gave her a faint smile.

She laughed. *Was he trying it on? What was going on in that head of his? Best not to think about it,* Hope reckoned.

She walked down the small stone path that led to the left-hand side of the block of four flats and realised from the number that Amanda Hughes's home was upstairs. Hope knocked on the door of the downstairs flat, stepped back and waited until a middle-aged man opened it.

'Hello. What can I do for you?' The man started to beam until he saw Hope pull out a warrant card.

'I'm Detective Sergeant Hope McGrath. I'm here to ask a few questions about the lady who lived upstairs.'

'Lived? She moved out?'

'No, sir. I'm afraid she's dead, but I'd like to ask you a few questions about her and her child.'

'Amanda is dead?' queried the man. 'When did that happen?'

'Yesterday sometime. Did you know her well, Mr . . . ?'

'Ian Lamb. I wouldn't say I knew her well. I mean, I have seen Amanda about. Nice enough person, would chat to me occasionally, you know, nothing exciting.'

'Did you know any of her friends?'

'No,' said Ian. 'I don't know how many she had either. I'd never seen anybody come back to the flat.'

'What about the block here? Who else lives downstairs and

upstairs?'

'Well, the Forsyths are next door, elderly couple. You know, they're all right. Upstairs has got a damp problem so nobody's been up there for, oh, nearly two years now. But you said she was dead. Was it something strange?'

'Why do you ask that?' queried Hope.

'Well, you're here asking questions. I just wondered, people often keel over and die. You don't tend to get the police pop in for questioning.'

The man is right, thought Hope. Yet something within her made her think that this man was worried about something.

'I'm just going to pop in and see the other neighbours downstairs,' said Hope. 'If you don't mind, can you hang about? I'll come back and ask a few questions. I just want to see if I can get a better picture of her. Maybe also see if I can get up and enter her flat.'

'Well, I don't have a key,' said Ian. 'I wasn't privy to any part of her life in that sense.'

Hope nodded, thanked the man, and walked round to the other side of the building, ringing the doorbell of the downstairs flat. An elderly woman, much smaller than Hope, with grey hair tightly permed, answered the door.

'Hello,' said the woman. 'Can I help you?'

'Who is it, dear?' came a voice from behind her.

'I don't know, I've just asked her.'

'Well, let her tell you then.'

'I'm trying to. Sorry, love. Who are you?'

'I'm Detective Sergeant Hope McGrath. I just want to ask you a few questions about one of your neighbours.'

'Ian Lamb? You've just being over there, haven't you?'

They were watching, thought Hope. *Watching out the window.*

'Why would you think I want to talk to Mr Lamb?'

'Well, you did,' said the woman. 'But he's a bit, isn't he?'

'A bit what?'

'Well, I think he had a crush on Amanda upstairs. You go and ask her.'

'I'm afraid I can't,' said Hope. 'Unfortunately, Amanda Hughes is deceased, as is her son.'

The woman's face went into shock. 'Both of them? Really? How?'

'Well, I'm not at liberty to say quite yet but we believe there was foul play abroad.'

'Amanda? But Amanda was . . . well, I mean, she didn't have it easy. Never easy but she was a decent girl. Looked after herself, looked after that kid. Money was tight for her, I know that. We used to give her the odd bit of food when we had stuff left over and that, but Ian was up there all the time. You should really ask him.'

'All the time?' queried Hope.

'Oh, he was forever up. I'm not sure she let him in the door, though. You could see him sometimes standing up the stairs or rather we heard the downstairs door being opened. Then she'd come down with him and try to shove him out the door really.'

'Is your husband there?' A head appeared from a door in the hallway where the man had clearly been listening.

'Hello,' said the man.

'Detective Sergeant Hope McGrath. I'm sorry to bother you, Mr Forsyth, but I'd be interested in your take.'

'Very much what the wife said. Amanda, I mean, she was a good-looking girl. Nothing dramatic but she had that nice kid. Just one of those people who had it hard, I guess. Ian is a man

39

on his own. I think probably he thought he could get in there. Nice little family set up already.'

'Was he ever in any way aggressive to her or obsessive?'

'No. She never complained about him. I don't think he ever got in the way. Talked a lot, but she was very polite like that. Amanda wouldn't have shooed anybody away, but she wasn't dumb either. I don't think she'd invited him into the house. Gave him any ideas.'

'Okay,' said Hope. 'Anything else you can tell me about her and her kid?'

'She took him to some of the clubs around here for the young ones. She'd also sometimes be with the mothers' group and that. There's a convent, isn't there? The nuns, I don't know if the nuns ever saw her. We don't really know. Actually, we don't go out like that much from here, except down to the bowling. He's always bowling. So, no, she was a good neighbour. Nothing more, nothing less to us.' said Mrs Forsyth.

Hope thanked them and then made her way back to the door of Ian Lamb and she rapped it again. She saw him open the door with his head down before lifting it slowly. 'I'd like to have a word with you, Mr Lamb, if that's possible. Can I come in?'

The man nodded. Hope saw his shoulders slump. He walked in and pointed to a kitchen table with a chair. 'You can take a seat if you want,' he said. 'Can I get you something?'

'It's fine,' said Hope. 'I just want some answers. When I was here earlier, you told me that you saw very little of Amanda, but, according to the Forsyths, you were always at her door chatting to her.'

Hope saw the man swallow hard. 'Well, I did like her, and I

thought she liked me; she gave me the key just in case she ever had problems or got locked out.'

'She trusted you enough to give you a key?' asked Hope.

'Oh, yes. I mean, the Forsyths are nosy busybodies. They're all right, but you wouldn't give them anything. They'd probably be up and inside your flat.'

'Have you ever been up inside Amanda's flat?'

'Well, I did want to. It's not easy. I haven't. Well . . .'

'What, Ian? What are you not telling me?'

'You see, I go to counselling. I get obsessed, fixated on people. I got a little bit fixated on Amanda. That's why I would chat to her all the time. You say she's dead?' Hope watched the man walk to the window of the kitchen and stare out. 'I can't believe she's dead. I mean, I was talking to her yesterday. Yesterday morning.'

'What was she saying?'

'Not a lot,' said the man. 'Not a lot.' Hope watched his feet as he began to bounce up and down on the balls of them.

'You seem to be shaking, Mr Lamb.'

'Yes,' he said. 'I am. She's gone. She's gone. What am I going to do?'

'Have you got the key to the flat?' asked Hope. 'Maybe we could go up. Have a look inside.'

'I have an obsession with her,' he said categorically. 'I've seen a counsellor and he helps me to keep it in check. I'm not violent or anything. I just like people and then I want to get close to them, I guess. I followed Amanda sometimes, you know? I know what you're thinking; she's dead and you're thinking this guy's probably done something. That's not me. I just get obsessed with people. There was somebody who was following her.'

41

'Keep talking,' said Hope.

'Well, I'd follow her about from a distance. She never saw me doing it.' The man was really shaking now and quite agitated, his face contorting at times when he spoke. 'The thing is that there was this man and he was often nearby. He was never with her, but I swore that he and her were having an affair or something. I think he was always there.'

'Can you describe him?' asked Hope.

'Taller than me. Six feet? What height are you?'

'I'm about six feet,' said Hope.

'Then six feet. He was your height. You know? Your height. Didn't look like you. Bald. He'd had a hat on often, but when he took it off, he was bald and thin. Not like you, not curved. Thin, not well built.'

Hope found it quite funny how the man would describe her as curved without any hint of sexual connotation from him.

'Did Amanda know you followed her?'

'No, but that man, I was never close to him. I never really saw his face because I had to keep my distance, too. I didn't want to frighten her. I didn't frighten her. I really never frightened her.'

'How do you know that?'

'Because, well, you see, I shouldn't really say—this is private.'

'Ian, if you know something, you need to tell me.'

'But it's private,' he said, the leg beginning to bounce again. 'Really private. I mean, as private as you can get.'

'What do you mean?' asked Hope. 'Do you mean—?'

'Three nights ago, I spent the night up there. She let me in, let us talk, and then, yes. Wow. It was . . . now she's dead. She's dead.' He turned and bent over double, tears flowing from his eyes. 'Why the hell is she dead? We were just getting together. We were just . . . We had . . . I don't understand. Why would someone? No.'

Part of Hope wanted to go over and console the man, but that would be wholly inappropriate as a sergeant investigating this case. Instead, she sat watching him, looked at him shake, asked him if he was okay, to which she was told he was bloody well not okay. 'How could anything be okay again?' she made a note that she needed to talk to his counsellor, but she also wanted to get up into Amanda's flat, and now she had a key.

Hope picked up her mobile phone and dialled Jona Nakamura's number, advising her that she needed a team to go through Amanda's flat. She also realised that the DNA of Mr Lamb would now be up there as well. He'd given her good cause. Looking at him, she wasn't sure if he was playing or he was genuinely this upset. She didn't have much experience in the field of dealing with people with these disorders if that's what he had.

'When you said you were up there, can you confirm with me you were having sexual intercourse with Amanda?'

'Of course not; it wasn't sex. It was love,' he said, eyes streaming with tears. 'It was love. She wasn't just some shag. I wasn't just some thing. We were bonded, bonded.'

The man sat down on his kitchen floor with his back up against one of the units, and wept into his hands. It would probably take Jona's team half an hour to get there, so Hope picked up her mobile again and called Macleod. She had a possible suspect, but only possible. A good part of her just didn't believe it.

Chapter 06

Clarissa Urquhart drove her green sports car onto the campus of Inverness University. It was bustling with students, but she was looking for a rather small department and a woman by the name of Claudia Wisecroft, Professor Wisecroft in fact, who was based in the history department and was the only local professor who was a specialist in symbology. Clarissa had made an appointment for that morning but noted that the woman was quite brisk with her on the telephone, as if Clarissa wasn't worth her time.

Arriving at the history department, Clarissa parked the car, walked into the front reception, and asked for Professor Wisecroft. The young receptionist picked up her phone and called to find no one on the other end of the line. She looked a little embarrassed and asked Clarissa if she would take a seat for a moment, and then disappeared off into the building. Some five minutes later, she returned.

'I'm sorry, but I can't find the professor anywhere. Oh, but hang on, there she is.'

Clarissa saw a small, dumpy woman with large glasses and her hair tied up in a bun behind her head. She reminded Clarissa of a friendly mother or grandma from a folktale.

44

Clarissa stood up, stretching out her hand towards the woman.

'Hi, I'm Detective Sergeant Clarissa Urquhart. I believe we have an appointment.'

'Quite right. It's good to see that you're on time. One doesn't like to be kept back.'

Flipping cheek, thought Clarissa. *You're late.*

'Is there somewhere we can talk privately?' asked Clarissa.

'If you would follow one up the stairs, I'll see if I can make room in one's office.'

She speaks rather strangely, thought Clarissa. *How far up herself could this woman be?*

Clarissa wasn't unused to people with a slight strangeness to them. In fact, many people said she was rather strange herself, but she was finding the professor to be a little bit off-putting. They marched up two flights of stairs before the professor opened a door into a small office with a wall full of books behind a desk. Here and there seemed to be knickknacks from all parts of the world, as well as a photograph of the professor meeting the queen, which was from many years ago, but had pride of place on the wall.

'Please, if you'll sit there and just explain how one can be of help to you, one will see what one can do.'

Will one? thought Clarissa. 'My name's Detective Inspector Clarissa Urquhart.'

'Come, come, you said that downstairs. Please, if you could expedite whatever it is we need to do.'

'Okay,' said Clarissa. Her back now up, she pulled an envelope out from within her shawl, took out several photographs from inside, and placed them on the table. The photographs showed the torso of the child who had died with all the symbols marked on him. Here and there were close-up images of

45

particular ones and Clarissa slapped them down on the table.

'We had a child murdered and when his body was found, these symbols were on it. I was hoping you might be able to identify some of them, and I don't mean the cross in the middle.'

'Of course, one can identify them. Sit down and give one a moment.'

Clarissa plunked herself down and stared at the woman as she bent over, looking at the symbols before her. Her glasses were taken in her right hand at times and moved up and down her nose as if she was focusing a magnifying glass. She was almost comical in the way that she shifted and several times her backside caught the chair behind her. Her crouch must have been painful. Clarissa couldn't see anyone remaining in that position for long.

'Anything?' asked Clarissa.

'Tut, tut, do not interrupt.' Her finger was held up and waved at Clarissa, at which she almost burst out laughing. *I'm near retirement*, thought Clarissa; *I'm actually near retirement. I'm no spring chicken and I am no university undergraduate. Where does she get off with this?* Knowing that she needed something from the woman, though, Clarissa kept shtum and continued to watch her closely.

The woman stood up, turned, and started delving into some books behind her. Several of them were placed open on the chair behind her. Then she went to the far end of her bookcase, grabbed a book, opened it, tutted, and dropped it on the floor when it proved unsatisfactory. She then marched back to the table, looked down at the photographs again, glasses extended back and forward on the nose before she looked up at Clarissa with almost a twinkle in her eye.

'I think you'll find that there's quite a number of symbols across different cultures. From one's examination, we can see a Mayan bat. The Mayan bat describes the underworld in their culture. We also have the upside-down cross, which no doubt you spotted. That's showing satanic connotations. The Amenta here,' she said, pointing at a symbol, 'and Duat, they are Egyptian underworld symbols. We also have a Norse Valknut.'

'So, what do they mean altogether?' asked Clarissa.

The woman shook her head. 'You wouldn't find these symbols together. They're from cultures from different parts of the world. To put them together is showing an ignorance of their meanings. They should be together with other local symbols, telling stories, giving an impression of maybe a funeral rite, or of what a building is, or maybe in a scroll, exercising what was to come in the next life. To place them together is random, and rather distressing, actually.'

Distressing? thought Clarissa. *How is that distressing compared to the child's body they're drawn on?*

'As I said, these symbols were found on a child. Carved, as you can see, delicately. Our pathologist says they would have had to be done with a steady hand, somebody trained at it. Are these symbols used anywhere else, in any particular cults or anything?'

The dumpy woman stood up straight, whipped the glasses off her nose, and stared at Clarissa. 'You wouldn't do that. Certainly, one wouldn't. It's too much of a mix. This is showing an obsession with death. Somebody, who I don't know, maybe understands little of the cultures, looked them up. What is it they say these days? Googled it. As to how well they carve, I can't answer that. Back in the days when

47

these things were being used, absolutely the satanic one is out of place. It's not about death, it's about anti-Christ, it's about being the opposite of that religion. The other ones are not, the other ones are part of the religious culture. Amenta, Duat, they're all part of the complex Egyptian gods. The Norse Valknut, the same. They're not anti. Death is not seen as anti in most cultures. It's seen as part of the cycle of life. To have a satanic cross in the middle, it seems wrong. Like the person didn't understand, had no concept of what they were really looking at.'

'So, if one were to suppose where these symbols were acquired from . . . ?'

'Like one said, online. If a student produced these to me altogether, I would have plenty to say to them. Poor research, poor understanding of the culture.'

'Could they be used, though,' asked Clarissa, 'by a sect or cult?'

'Of course, they could. Cultures adapt other cultures' symbols lots of times. The Christian Church has adopted symbols, Christmas trees, rings, from other cultures. Many cultures do that, too. After a while, they don't even realise that it's from a different culture. That's one of the things about cultures—they develop; they grow.'

'Have you seen these symbols anywhere recently? Has there been any instance of them being used in a nefarious manner as opposed to archaeological digs? Historical evidence.'

'Outside of the satanic cross? One is not aware of any such instance.'

'I guess what I'm trying to ask is, is there any known cult that uses these symbols?'

'One can look for you, but one can't say at the moment

whether that is the case. One appreciates, Sergeant, that this is rather disturbing. The death of a child would certainly want to be explained, but I can't explain this, frankly, abhorrent use of these symbols, and I don't just mean that because the child had them carved into it. More to the point that they're just used so far out of context.'

Clarissa was struggling to come to terms with how the woman was feeling so angry about the symbols rather than the death of the child, but such as it was, she still needed the professor.

'Would you be able to put down what these symbols are with a brief history for me and send it over to my email?'

'One can probably find the time. When would you like it for?'

'Today, please,' said Clarissa. 'And if anyone comes calling from the press, or anywhere outside of Inverness police, then please, not a word. No one as yet knows beyond our team about the symbology. We don't want it going any further and causing hysteria.'

'Of course, one can perfectly understand how the simple mind will get worked up about these symbols, instead of understanding a lot of them for what they are.'

I was actually thinking because they were on the body of a child, thought Clarissa, *but as long as she takes the point.* Clarissa reached her hand over. 'Thank you, professor. If anything else occurs with similar such symbology, I will come to you again, if that's okay.'

'Of course. You'll need to consult an expert, and an expert here you have. I wish you all the best with your investigation, Sergeant.'

Clarissa left a card on the professor's desk which detailed her phone number and her email address before acknowledging the professor once again and leaving her office. Once outside, Clarissa fought against the feeling that this woman could have been some sort of fraud. Certainly, her voicing was. She tried to speak like she was royalty. Clarissa gave a laugh, but as she then walked out back to her little green sports car, she pondered on what the woman had said. *Random selection of symbols.* If someone had picked symbols deliberately, it'd be easier to trace.

Was this just some delaying tactic, some way of disguising what was really going on? Was it simple murder, and then these symbols were there to throw her off the case? Or did the symbols actually mean something to somebody else? Had they formed their own cult, some way of pretending to be something?

They'd taken death from every culture, but in those cultures, death wasn't seen as an enemy, as a bad thing. They'd slapped a satanic cross in the middle of it, the Anti-Christ view. Her head began to swim with the symbols, and as she sat down in her sports car, she breathed deeply. *Poor kid*, she thought. *That poor kid. What sick bastard turns around and starts carving on a kid's body?*

Clarissa had seen plenty in the art world. Brutal people who would kill for a painting, people who would kill anyone else just for a piece of artwork. While she loved her art, she recognised it was there to lift up humanity, to make it better, to help it understand itself. Not there as some sort of commodity. She had hoped going to the professor would've given them a culture to chase after, someone with an interest in one of those South American places. Now she didn't have that.

Where did you go? You couldn't find someone with an interest in just generally everything, and if that was the case, the professor was the main suspect. She hoped that McGrath was having a better time of it. She went to start the car but stopped, reached up, and wiped a tear from her eye. Coming to the murder squad had been hard. She'd started to see more bodies, but this one had physically made her throw up, and want to throw up again. Even thinking back to it now, she wanted to step out of the car. Well, as undignified as it would be, she wasn't going to let that happen.

Focus, she thought. *You have to focus on the task, not on what's happened.* Clarissa turned the key in the ignition, reached up again, and took another wipe at her eye. At least she had something to go back with for Macleod. They may not understand why the symbols were there, but at least she understood what they were, and that was a start. And that was the point, wasn't it? Get started.

Chapter 07

Hope McGrath stayed at the flat of Ian Lamb, while upstairs the forensic unit went through Amanda Hughes's flat with a fine-tooth comb. For his part, Lamb remained plonked on the kitchen floor, half sobbing, half weeping, constantly shaking. Macleod had appeared as well, saying he was up to his eyes with those above him looking for information.

Already, it felt like the pressure was on, and he got called away before forensics were finished. He had joined Hope for a brief re-interview of Ian Lamb, as much to have his own opinion on the man and compare it to Hope's. She wasn't annoyed that he'd done that. It was reasonable practice. The two of them learned that it was best to have at least two opinions on something, but each one seemed to match up.

There was a knock at the front door of Ian's flat. Hope heard the door being opened by a constable and she saw the familiar figure of Jona Nakamura. She was dressed in a white coverall and had one in her hand for Hope.

'I think it's time we took a look upstairs,' she said, and then glanced across at the man sitting on the kitchen floor. She said nothing, merely stared at him before giving a little flick of her head, indicating Hope should follow. Once they were outside the flat, Jona stared up at her taller colleague. 'Get ready for this one.'

'Get ready for what?' asked Hope.

'I'm not spoiling the surprise.'

With that, the Asian woman disappeared over to the door for the upper flat. Hope climbed the stairs behind her. It had a dark brown carpet, one that seemed to have been there for years, for it was threadbare in places. The walls were magnolia, as if someone hadn't been bothered to go out and pick a proper colour. There was a single light at the top of the stairs which had no shade on it. Once you got to the top, there were two doors on either side. One was lying open.

'Through here.'

Jona led Hope into what was a large lounge. There was a TV at the far end which looked an older model. The furniture inside also was quite aged, maybe picked up from a charity shop. Certainly not from one of the modern furniture stores. Here and there she saw pictures of Steven, the child who had died. He seemed to be smiling in most pictures. In some, he was a baby. Here and there, she would see Amanda with him. There weren't any pictures of anyone else, though. No grandparents, no siblings, no one else, just Steven and Amanda.

'Did you find anything else?' asked Hope.

'Follow me.'

Jona led Hope into the kitchen. Again, everything seemed normal. There was a microwave, a small gas cooker, a cheap table at which maybe two or three people could sit down to eat.

'All seems fairly regular, doesn't it?' said Jona. 'Come on.' She took her on a tour of the bathroom, containing a tub with candles around it. Here and there, a dressing gown, one for the child, one for her, some tiles stacked up at the wall.

'What do you notice about the location of the bathroom and the bedroom?' asked Jona.

Hope looked around her. 'Well,' she said, 'the living room is on the outside, so you've got the window on the far side. Kitchen is outside too, but you come to the bedroom, you're more to the centre of the house, as is the bathroom.'

'Indeed,' said Jona. 'Which means that the bedroom and the bathroom run side to side with the other upper flat. Did they build them that way, sort of mirror images?'

'They did, far as I know?'

'Do you know anything about the other flat?' asked Jona.

'Not a lot. Why?'

'Come with me,' said Jona. She led her back out onto the original upper landing that had the two doors for each flat. She walked over to the other flat where the door swung open easily when Jona pushed it. Hope nearly backed away from the smell.

'Dear God, that stinks,' she said, looking around at a room that had mildew inside.

'This living room is unreal, isn't it,' said Jona, but Hope thought she looked almost impassive to the smell. The sofa had a fungus growing on it, the walls, too. 'Terrific amount of damp, isn't there,' said Jona.

'How do you not notice this from the outside?'

'Wait till you see the rest of the place.'

Jona led Hope through to the kitchen, which didn't seem as bad even though there was some damp, but then through to the bedroom and the bathroom. Each of these was pristine. More than that, lying on the bedroom floor was a large amount of pornographic material, all blonde-haired models.

'Looks like a carpet was not required.' Hope stared at the material, realising that some of it had been stained and really didn't want to think about how. 'Hang on a minute,' she said. 'How do we get from a mess like what's out there in the living room, to the mess of what's in here?' she bent down but Jona told her not to touch.

'We're not done going through here, but I thought you needed to see it. Do you notice anything about the photographs?' said Jona.

Hope looked down at the magazine cut-outs, one after another. 'They're all blonde. None of them are really, really young, are they? They're all sort of middle-aged women or women in their thirties.'

'Exactly,' said Jona. 'They've all got a certain look. Same look as I saw on that woman who was pulled out of the river.'

'They do,' said Hope. 'You're right, they do. This is obsessive.'

'And watch this,' said Jona as she stepped forward towards the wall of the bedroom where there was a picture up. When she lifted it off, there was a small hole.

'This is really cleverly cut,' she said. 'If you look through it, you might see one of my team.'

Hope walked over as Jona stepped away, put her eye up to the hole in the wall. Lo and behold, inside was indeed one of Jona's team in the bedroom of Amanda Hughes's flat. There were also holes in the bathroom.

'So, it's just like some sort of perving suite. Blimey. I mean . . .'

'What do you know about up here?' asked Jona. 'Because see that front room, that's not a leak; that's not something that's been left over time. Somebody has gone in there and actually

55

wet the inside. The mildew, it's not in the woodwork, it's not in the floors. It's all on the surface of the items in there. There is not damp coming in from the outside. The damp has been introduced to the room. Somebody has gone up with a bucket or a hose and they have made sure everything in there is wet.'

'They've made it wet so that people will keep out. You've got to the door, you push open, it stinks. Then you've got in here where you can just . . . well, what would you call it?'

'Playtime?' said Jona. 'Pervert's paradise. I mean, I wouldn't have thought much of it in the sense that maybe somebody has a wee peephole like that, but the material on the floor says that's an obsession with the person next door. Somebody is obsessed with Amanda.'

'I have somebody sat downstairs who's obsessed with Amanda,' said Hope. 'Shakes when talking about it. I think I need to talk to him again. You said you haven't gone over this yet?'

'No, but if we get some DNA from the man downstairs, there's . . . how do I put it? . . . DNA on some of this material. We'll see if it's a match.'

Hope nodded, watching where she put her feet as she left the room. Having retreated downstairs and taken off her white overall, Hope returned to the kitchen of Ian Lamb.

'You haven't been telling me everything, have you, Ian?' said Hope as she entered the kitchen. 'You told me the upstairs flat next to Amanda's was full of damp.'

'It is. Open the door and smell it.'

'I did open the door and I did smell it. My good friend Jona says, however, that somebody has gone in there with a bucket or hose and soaked the place to make it damp. Jona also took a trip beyond that room, a trip into the bedroom and the bathroom upstairs, the one that links into Amanda's side-to-side, wall-to-wall. And do you know what, Ian? Somebody's cut a peephole through.'

The man looked away, but he started to shake again.

'Were you gawking on her? Were you watching her?'

Ian began to shake, and then he stood up, nervously gripping hold of the kitchen sideboard. 'She's lovely, isn't she? She was lovely. I mean, you don't understand. I was just admiring her. I was just enjoying the view. I didn't want to harm her. I went up there several times.'

'More than several times, judging by what was on the floor.'

'They were a pale imitation. I had them down here and then the owner died. Old man. I wasn't sure if he had anybody and then the flat never got sorted, so I went up there one day, got in and realised it was next door. I used to sit in the bedroom and I could hear her. I told my counsellor this, I said to him, I think I'm obsessed with her. The good thing about counsellors is that they don't tell anyone.'

'But you told him about drilling the holes through, did you? Told him about that?'

The man went silent. 'No,' he said. 'He would've reported that. I told him I bought some magazines with women who were like her, and then I was up in that flat next to her. But I never told him about the holes because he would've said that was wrong. He would've said I shouldn't have done that. He would've said don't, and then I wouldn't have seen her.'

Hope felt a chill run through her and yet something else was striking her. This man, he was . . . something not right. He clearly was having difficulty.

'When was the last time you were up there?' Hope asked him.

'Week ago,' he said. 'She had been out at the doctors, I think, or something. She came back and she had a bath. Then I could tell you what she did in the bedroom.'

'No,' said Hope. 'You were there a week ago. Why only a week ago?'

'Because then she invited me up and we went to bed together. You don't do that to your partner, do you? You don't do those sorts of things.'

'Ian, you don't do that sort of thing to somebody who's not your partner either,' said Hope. 'You say you never told your counsellor any of this?' The man shook his head. 'I'm going to need his number because I think we're going to need him at the moment, aren't we?'

The man was clearly a vulnerable adult, someone with a serious problem, a problem that probably wasn't fully understood. Maybe one that seemed a lot less dangerous than it did to her right now. She would have to check the register, see if he was on it. She left him in the room with a constable watching over, but she stepped outside to think about what was next. After a few minutes, she came back inside.

'Where were you yesterday?'

'Why?' asked the man. 'Why do you want to know? I don't tell these things. I don't tell people.'

'What do you mean you don't tell people?'

'I don't tell people where I go.'

'Were you waiting about, Ian?' asked Hope. 'Did you see Amanda yesterday?'

'I saw her. Yes, I saw her.'

'What did you think of Steven?' she asked.

'He liked her. He really did. Sometimes, he would come into her bedroom, and they'd cuddle.'

'Well, she was his mum,' said Hope.

'He had a special relationship. I wanted that. I wanted the relationship. Special. One where I would be the one she'd wanted.'

'Did you see Steven as in the way?'

'The way of what?'

'The way of you getting into that relationship.'

'They don't have any of them. They don't have any kids in the relationships.'

'Who doesn't?'

'The women in the magazines. They're just there.'

Hope had a very chill feeling running through her. She had no concrete evidence that this man was a major suspect. Yet there was also the claim he made of the other man that was following her. Was that delusional?

Hope picked up the phone and called Macleod. They needed to come together and work this out. Maybe they'd stopped everything before it had begun, but with this man, what was there to begin?

After speaking to Macleod and asking for him to come together for a conference, she walked back into the kitchen and watched Ian now sitting there on the floor, still crying, still shaking. There was a doubt in the back of her mind. He looked too good, too perfect, too ideal. Sometimes that was the case, wasn't it? Sometimes that just was the case. Macleod would know. Yes, Seoras would know.

Chapter 08

The team had gathered back at the Inverness police station to take stock of the situation. Macleod was pacing around his office, waiting for them to gather and for Jona to join in. She had been looking at the post-mortems of the bodies, delayed in getting to them. Despite that, Macleod was happy.

There was a possible conclusion to the case, albeit he wasn't entirely convinced yet. The DCI, when he'd updated him, was also pleased, and was ready to go to the press with news that someone had been picked up. Yes, at the moment, Ian Lamb was only helping with inquiries. Macleod thought it unwise to go to the press with anything until someone was formally arrested. Until that time, the process would continue. Macleod would keep working with the evidence along with the team.

The day, however, had been a good one. Hope had got on with things. Clarissa was getting somewhere on the symbology, and they had a potential suspect. In many cases, they hadn't got this far so quickly. As he looked at the darkness outside and the lights of Inverness shining, Macleod felt he was in a good place. He'd spoken recently to Jane saying he'd be back that night. That was the other thing that bothered him—staying out so long in the thrust and cut of these investigations and the first few days where he'd barely sleep. When he did, he was usually in a chair somewhere. He was grateful that tonight, he'd be back in his own bed.

There came a knock at his door. He turned to see it opening, and Hope McGrath stepping inside. The tall sergeant still had her red hair tied up but she had a grin on her face.

'Jona's just coming; are you ready for her, Seoras?'

'As soon as you're ready. Come on in. Grab a seat. I'll just go and do the coffee.'

'Ross is already on that.'

'Of course, he is,' said Macleod. 'He's always on it. Clarissa here, too?'

Hope was suddenly pushed to one side. In marched the tour de force that was Clarissa Urquhart.

'Of course, I'm here. I want to go home, been up on my feet all day. Still, it's looking good, Seoras, isn't it?'

'He's looking good, but let's keep the professionalism until we get into cars to go home.'

Clarissa nodded and he could see that she was obviously cold for she still had her shawl around her. She would often complain to him about the offices going cold later in the evening. *It was ridiculous that they weren't heated then, especially when they had to work through the night.* Macleod had no idea what she was talking about. The place always felt warm. Sometimes too warm, but always warm to him.

Ross arrived with a tray of coffee and set, it down on the table, each cup placed in front of the seat that the cup owner belonged to. They now had a well-established pattern around the table and Jona's seat was left free as they sat down.

61

'She's definitely on her way over?' queried Macleod.

'Give her a moment,' said Hope, testily. They took a couple of quick sips and Macleod looked over at Ross.

'Any more on your development?'

'I guess as I said, been too busy myself to check it up, sir.'

'Probably won't hear for a while, eh?'

'Probably not, sir.' Macleod thought Ross was rather flat about the whole thing. He hoped that what the man had seen recently wasn't putting him off the idea of parenthood.

Jona Nakamura swept into the room, dressed in a black jumper and dark jeans. She plonked herself down almost abruptly and untied her hair from behind, letting it drape over her shoulders.

'Let's get going,' she said.

Macleod stared at her from the other end of the table. 'I'm sure that's my line, but of course. The current situation is that we have a main suspect in Ian Lamb. We want to run through to make sure that he is where we want to be targeting at the moment.'

'Shall I start on the DNA front, Inspector?' asked Jona.

Again, Macleod felt a little rushed, but he acquiesced. 'By all means, Jona.'

'We checked through Amanda Hughes's house. There's definitely DNA from Ian Lamb there and on the bed. He's not lying when he talked about going to bed with her. The flat next door, it's him too. His DNA is all over that bedroom that he used to spy on her. It's also in the bathroom.'

'When you say it's in the bedroom?' asked Macleod.

'It's in the residue he left behind from his actions,' Jona said delicately.

'No one else's?'

'What are you on about?' asked Clarissa. 'You think that it's some sort of club up there?'

'No. Just covering the bases,' said Macleod. 'The idea that one man would do that's bad enough.'

'You're right; it gives me the creeps,' said Clarissa. She shuddered underneath her shawl.

'There's only one type of DNA in that empty flat and that is Ian Lamb. It looks like he set it up and protected it by making the front room seem so full of damp and mildew that nobody would have gone in anyway.'

'Surely somebody would have found out at some point,' said Clarissa. 'You can't keep on going on like that. Somebody would have bought it.'

'Apparently not. No new bills lying around,' said Jona. 'Nor a householder around. I'm not sure how far down the road the counsellor got with dealing with Ian.'

'Looks like he called it quits some time ago,' Clarissa murmured. Macleod gave her a look as if she should pipe down.

'Let's keep going then. We know Ian Lamb's telling the truth in that he operated a peeping den on Amanda Hughes. We know he did go to bed with her at some point. We confirmed from his counsellor what he's getting counsel for.'

'Yes,' said Hope. 'I had a conversation today. It appears that the counsellor thought that Ian had an obsessive nature. He didn't see him as a threat, however. Apparently, Ian's never been a threat to anyone, but he does obsess over certain people. As he went into adult life, he obsessed over women every now and again. It would be a particular one, but he's never done anything to them. Never even acted inappropriately towards one.'

'Only done it from the shadows,' said Macleod. 'It was quite a big effort up there though, wasn't it?'

'I mentioned this to the counsellor, and he said the opportunity obviously developed for him. He says a crush for a woman for Ian was strong. The problem is that part of it is a real and genuine feeling for her. Some of it though, as I have seen, has a lot of self-gratification involved in it.'

'Didn't he have the opportunity though, to kill?' asked Macleod.

'Ian says he was asleep,' said Hope. 'He'd been upstairs the previous night, and he obviously slept with her, but he hadn't seen her on that day for he slept on and she was gone by the time he got up. He's got no one to say he was in his flat; he's got no one to say he was anywhere else. The time frame for when Amanda Hughes was murdered means that Ian Lamb could have done it. We can't rule him out.'

'Still circumstantial, isn't it?' said Macleod. 'Yes, we got a man who clearly wants Amanda Hughes but nothing to say he wants her in that way.'

'Well, what about the symbols?' asked Clarissa. 'Is he in any way involved in a cult? Any way involved with anything like that? Occult ideas?'

'Well, I've been going through his computer records,' said Ross. 'There's nothing occult in there. I can't find anywhere in his computer where he's checked into any chat room involving that type of symbology or anything that would involve ritual sacrifices, even simple rituals at all. To be honest, his computer life basically mirrors what he was doing in the upstairs flat. Lots of pictures of women, usually blonde, usually in their thirties. He's obsessed with a woman of that form.'

'So,' said Macleod, 'we have a man who clearly wanted Amanda Hughes, to the point that he's obsessed with her. He's slightly unstable. However, he also got what he wanted. Why would he take her and her son, killing the son, carving symbols on him and then ditch Amanda as well. Why would he kill the pair of them when he just got the very thing he wanted? I'm not seeing anything that's saying he's a killer. We might believe him to be a pervert, we might believe him to be a seriously ill person with major issues around how he deals with relationships, but I'm not seeing anything that says that he killed anyone. We didn't find any evidence in his house that he had ornate knives. Are we still working on the wounds, Jona, for what the weapon would have been?'

'I believe it's a curved knife,' said Jona. 'I believe from the type of wounds that the knife is curved and it's probably very delicate. Very thin, as well.'

'I'm beginning to feel this isn't an open and shut case,' said Hope, 'We've got an awful lot on the man, but like you said, Seoras, it's all circumstantial. None of it is solid evidence. We hunted for the knife in his flat; we couldn't find it. Hunted in the upstairs flat; couldn't find it. We've had officers going into the river looking for it and haven't found it. Everything just seems a little bit strange.'

'That it does,' agreed Macleod, 'but I'm inclined to hold him anyway at the moment. Hold him for his own good. He seems very unstable since learning of her death.'

'He sat on the floor for hours weeping. They couldn't get him to move,' said Hope. 'He was devastated. If it was an act, it was a heck of an act.'

'Well, it has been known,' said Clarissa. 'It has been known that people do things that they then detach themselves from it and take the grief that came from being a bystander. We did say he's somewhat unhinged.'

'Let's be careful what we're saying about him. He's not just somebody nuts; he has specific issues,' said Macleod. 'We don't want to cross the lines here. It's one thing being a murderer with a need to kill; it's another thing for being unable to express your feelings correctly or know and understand what you feel for someone.'

'What do we do then, boss?' asked Hope.

'I think the best thing we can do is call it a night, start again in the morning. I'm not happy that there's no symbology coming out in the life of Ian Lamb; there's no connection to these symbols. We need to go somewhere with the symbols. That's on you, Clarissa. As for tonight. I think we all go home now, get a good night's sleep, come back refreshed. Thank you, Jona, for your efforts.'

Jona stood up gave a nod and then raced off quickly. Macleod stared after her as the rest of the team stood up.

'She got something on, Hope?'

'No. New boyfriend, meant to be going out tonight for dinner with friends. Probably hoping to catch the last of them.'

'Okay, but it's like ten o'clock at night. Where do you go for dinner at ten o'clock at night? I don't eat then.'

'It's a slightly different world, I think, sir.'

Macleod looked up at Ross. 'Are you saying I'm old?'

'I don't think anyone has to say it, Seoras.' Clarissa was always ready with a cutting comment. She was older than he. 'You fancy a curry though?' she asked.

'Getting back to Jane,' said Macleod. 'Since this kicked off, she hasn't seen any signs of me. Few quick phone calls, that's been it. At least I can go home to snore beside her for a couple of hours.'

Hope seemed to laugh but Clarissa simply gave a nod and

began to walk from the room. As Ross got up, Macleod went over to him.

'Ross, if you need anything with regards to the application, if you need some time when this is going on, you just say. You can't screw up that side of your life just because you were off here, running around doing detective work. We'll back you up as far as we can.'

'That's kind of you, sir, but if you need me, I'm here.' Macleod put out his hand and Ross questioningly took it.

'Just wanted to say best of luck with it. I may not have been the best witness to her but all the best. I only spoke honestly when I said I had no idea if two men would make a good father, or a good set of parents. I genuinely don't know but I've seen enough male and female parents come together and make a botch of the job. I also speak without experience.'

'I think sometimes you speak too much, sir,' said Ross. 'Sometimes it's maybe better to say you just don't know.'

The man shook Macleod's hand and disappeared. Even Macleod wondered if he'd done right by the man. Macleod's phone began to ring, and as Hope was on the other side of the table, gave her a nod to answer it. As he walked over to pick up his coat from the hanger by the door, he heard the tone in Hope's voice begin to get sharper.

'When? Still there? We will be right down.' Macleod gazed at her as she put the phone down and turned to him.

'It's happened again, Seoras. It's another one.'

Chapter 09

S andy's head pounded. It felt like somebody had put a little gnome inside of her, one that was dancing on her brain, kicking at it. Thump, thump, thump. She could just lie here, lie here and accept it. Except she couldn't anymore. Six, seven years ago she could. Six, seven years ago it was just her, no one else. Then Britney had happened.

Britney had been the result of a manufacturer's defect in a male contraceptive device. Britney was the result of an accident, although Sandy would never tell her that. It was an accident that had changed Sandy's life from one where she could do whatever she wanted to one where Britney was always pulling her away from what she wanted to do.

Responsibilities, she'd faced up to them. She had kept Britney, not sent her away, despite the fact that the man who had bought the defective device, Britney's father, had disappeared a long time ago. Yes, he'd given the odd promise of money, a promise that he'd be around, but in truth he wasn't. And then she'd struggled to get work, gave up, and stayed on benefits.

Well, benefits and a few extras that she did. She wasn't proud of them, but at the end of the day it paid well, and it allowed

Sandy to go out on occasion. Britney was all right as long as she stayed within the house. The TV was more than a good babysitter. She loved those shows, and now with channels being available nearly twenty-four hours a day, she sat glued to them.

That's what had happened last night. Last night she'd gone out. It had been over a week since she'd had, and the bottles of wine in the house hadn't sated her appetite. She liked to go dancing. Thump, thump, thump like the little gnome in her head, pounding her way around the floor, sweating it up and dropping the odd pill. These were good times when she disappeared off somewhere away from here, away from this crappy home, but last night, she'd come back with someone. She was sure of it; there'd been someone in there.

Sandy put her right hand out, feeling around the bed. There was no one there now. She put her left arm out and she was unsure of where she was in the bed, but it fell off the end into space and she flapped around momentarily before bringing it back up to her side. She must have had someone come back with her. Surely. After all, she wasn't wearing anything. She didn't do that normally.

Sandy had a collection of fun pyjamas that she liked to wear, some of them extremely warm. If she brought someone back, she wouldn't have brought them out. She must have, must have been with someone.

Wonder where he is, she thought. *It would've been a 'he', wouldn't it?* She wasn't that far gone. She remembered being on the dance floor. She remembered the man smiling at her. Well, she remembered a smile, though not too sure what he looked like. There were a couple of pills. *There were pills, weren't there?*

Sandy opened her eyes, and tried to scan around the room,

wondering if maybe he was standing watching her, or trying to dress quietly and slip off. The light was bright though. It was about time that bedside light began to work properly. All these new-fangled bulbs, they never showed enough light, did they? But it did now.

Sandy reached down for her covers, realising they'd only gone halfway up her back, and then sat up in the bed. She grabbed her head and felt like it was going to fall off, and then she noticed the curtains were wide open in the bedroom.

Sandy had a ground floor flat. People walked past, which was why she never kept the curtains open when she was in the bedroom. She lurched out of the bed, racing over to close them quickly, and then realised that she'd discarded the rest of the bed covers and was now closing the curtains with nothing on. She peered outside from behind them. No one was there.

Thank goodness, she thought. She stumbled over to the set of drawers that occupied the other side of the bedroom, pulled out the top one, and slipped on a pair of knickers. She thought about socks, but then she shoved the drawer closed again, pulled open the one beneath and hauled on a pair of tracksuit bottoms. A drawer further down gave up a t-shirt. *That would do it for the moment*, she thought. *After all, I'm just going to wander through, see if I can find Britney. See if she's all right, maybe get her some breakfast.*

Sandy stopped. Why was it so bright outside? Breakfast time wasn't bright. Breakfast at this time of year was, well, the change, wasn't it? The dawn coming through. That sort of red hue some days, the days when you could start to see, but, actually, everything's not that clear.

She fumbled around on the bedside dresser until she found a pair of glasses and slipped them on. As she did so, the world became less blurred, and she looked at the bed. Someone had slept there last night! She stopped for a moment. How did she feel? Had they? Well, they must have had, hadn't they? If they came back, they didn't just lie beside her and crash out. If they were coming back with her, they were coming back for something, some sort of excitement.

She couldn't remember any of it though, which was a pity. Sometimes it was a good memory. She looked again at the bed. No, nobody had lain there, had they? Why'd she thought that? That was the undercover. The bed had two sheets on the bottom, and then the duvet. Where was the middle sheet? Somebody had laid there. The other sheet was removed, leaving the little ruts that would fit a figure sleeping in it. It was all too much currently, after such a night. What time was it anyway, seven? Sandy stared in shock at the clock. How did it get to seven?

She wandered through to the kitchen, turned on the tap, took a cup and drank a glass of water. Half of it spilled down her top as her hands shook. What was up with her? Maybe it was a bad tablet, although she didn't get many of those. Usually she felt fine; she'd be dehydrated though. You didn't get to dance like that, sweating away, without losing a few pounds of fluid. Still, she'd better go find Britney, wherever she was in the flat.

Sandy traipsed through to the small bedroom, but she wasn't there. In fact, her bed hadn't even been slept in. The covers were still there, as she'd made them. She told Britney to get to bed not past eleven. Britney was never up before her. The kid liked to sleep, but then she stayed up late like her mum.

Sandy padded on through to the bathroom. *No, Britney hadn't fallen asleep in there either. Where was she then?* Sandy's

71

heart began to beat. *Well, sometimes she plays outside, doesn't she?* She looked over and saw the clock on the wall.

Seven p.m.? It wasn't seven in the morning, but seven at night. How did that happen?

Something's up. Something's wrong, she thought. She raced to the front door in her bare feet, stepped down onto the concrete beyond and looked up and down, but there was no sign of Britney. She knocked next door and the old man answered, Jameson. He had moved in a couple of years ago and he was always good. If he saw Britney in trouble, he helped her. Sometimes he'd look after her before bringing her back. Sweet old dear.

'Have you seen her?' asked Sandy. She desperately watched the man's face.

'No,' he said, 'I haven't seen her all day. I thought you were holed up in there. You must have had a rough night if you're up now.'

'Must have been. I think I came back with someone. Not sure though. I'll go have a wander around. Sometimes she likes to play out in her den.'

'Well, let me know if you don't find her.'

Sandy thanked the man and turned around. Once inside, she wrapped herself up in a large coat, put on a pair of trainers and stepped back out into the evening. The sky was beginning to darken. Britney knew she wasn't meant to be outside when it got dark. She should be back unless she'd fallen asleep in the den.

Quickly, Sandy walked round, past the various parking spaces beside the flats to the hedge at the rear. Beyond the hedge was a railway line, but if you followed along on this side, you got to a point in the hedge where it became thicker, and Britney had made a hole for herself in it. Sandy crouched down on her knees, ignoring the cold of the muck, reached inside with her hand and found a blanket that Britney normally sat on.

'Britney?' she said. 'You in there, pet?' There was nothing. Sandy could feel her heart beginning to pound more. *That's where she would go, surely.* There was no one so she walked back alongside the railway track and back into the car park. *Maybe she'd gone off to the play park. It wasn't that far.* Sandy traipsed along the streets until she found the play park at the centre of the estate. There were some teenagers kicking about and she marched up to them, asking them if they'd seen the little girl.

'No,' said one of the boys and then gave her a wolf whistle. Sandy didn't have time for that. She turned but then the boy stepped forward, putting his hand on her shoulder.

'Piss off,' she said and slapped him with the back of her hand. She'd clearly done it with enough power and venom because he backed off. 'There's been no little girls around here. There's no need for that,' he said. 'You looked the type.'

Sandy marched off. That was the problem, wasn't it? She did look the type but worse, some days she was the type. She walked back to the house, hoping that Britney had made it back, but when she re-entered, there was no one there. When she stepped back outside to talk again to the old man next door, it was fully dark.

'That's not too good. We'll have another hunt around,' he said. 'No point getting the police yet, is there?'

No, there wasn't, thought Sandy. The last thing she needed was the police. She didn't get on with them. They were always hunting here and there, taking away your stash. She couldn't afford to have her stash taken. She didn't have enough money to replace it. Then she nodded in agreement and the pair of them split up in opposite directions, Sandy this time returning to the hedge at the rear of the flats, following the railway line further down towards where the river would be.

She stepped out from the hedge to the car park of the flats further down where there was a row of garages. Sometimes she might run in and out of here, try and see if any were open, pop herself inside. Sandy bent down, gently testing each one. None opened. She stumbled as she got to the end, to the dark side of the garages where the streetlights were obscured. She turned, put her hand on the wall, feeling along as the dark was more prevalent and then nearly tripped over something.

What was that? She reeled backwards, stepping away from the wall. She struggled to focus and the next thing, she pulled out her mobile phone, activating the light on the back of it. Holding it up in front of her, the first thing she saw was a pair of small bare legs. Then, there was a torso pinned to the wall, hands held back too. As the light went higher, she saw what should have been Britney's smiling face. Instead, the child's head was tipped forward, but her eyes were closed and, in some ways, she looked peaceful, the hair falling down on either side. Her body was limp, but something had attached her shoulders to the wall and the arms drooped off the torso limply like the head.

Sandy felt the vomit rising to the back of her throat and then turned away, unleashing upon the pavement a cascade. She turned around again, screamed as the light passed over the torso of the child and she saw the deep cuts. It was like she'd been tattooed but not with paint, not with a colouring needle. Instead, it was like she'd simply been the canvas on which to work, to cut out.

Sandy fell to her knees, screaming again, wailing loudly. So much so that there was a panic amongst people nearby. She heard the footsteps of her neighbour running towards her but she couldn't see him. Her eyes were so wet with tears, everything became a blur, a merciful blur in the case of Britney.

'Oh, dear God,' said a voice beside her. It was her neighbour and he dropped to one knee throwing his arms around her, holding her, telling her he was so, so sorry. Britney was gone. *Gone,* she thought.

Chapter 10

Macleod lifted his feet, weary as he was, and trudged along the line of garages to the end, where he saw the familiar white coverall of Jona Nakamura. He was dressed in his own, the shoes covered as well, and she waved him close. Unlike the gloom further back along the garages, this end was now lit up with incredibly bright beams that only threw in to stark contrast the tableau he saw before him.

The child was somehow supported on the wall, and he didn't know how at this time, but a pair of shoulders sagged forward which left the arms dangling, the head tipping forward as well. He saw the marks on the body, those symbols cut again. The one in the middle, the upside down cross, seemed to nod, seemed to almost mock him, as if it was his fault that he hadn't managed to stop this in time. From behind him, his tall sergeant stepped around, stood beside Jona, and then reduced a considerable size difference by crouching down.

'Similar to the last one, Seoras, very similar.'

'Yes, it is,' said Macleod. 'I take it the cuts are the same depth?'

'Very much so,' said Jona. 'At least as far as I can tell from this distance. Obviously, when we get back to the lab, we'll be able to be much more accurate. Same style to a large degree, but if you look at them, the symbols aren't cut as well. I don't know if it's the same knife even. I can't tell if it's the ineptitude of the carver or if it's the lack of a good knife.'

Macleod felt like taking a step back, taking himself out of this world. They seemed to talk about things as if what was in front of them wasn't real. *The lack of a good knife*, he thought, *as if you just buy these things in the corner shop.* 'I take it the mother hasn't been back to see again?'

'No,' said Jona. 'They've kept her away. Must have been hell for her.'

'We're going to go and interview her next then,' said Hope.

'Yes,' said Macleod. 'Yes, we shall.' His heart felt heavy. There was nothing to do here in terms of saving anyone. All they could do was learn what they could, move on and see if they could find the culprit, stop this before it became another murder. He knew his instincts were right the first time he saw the carvings on young Steven. Now here she was, Britney. Macleod shook his head and then tried to steady himself, looking closely at the body, looking for detail, for motive, for anything really. They were so out on a limb now, nowhere near where this investigation would be solved.

'We'll get him, Seoras. We'll get him, or her.'

It must have been written over his face. Well, Hope could read him now. It was true, though, what they said. When it was children, it was different. The way it touched you, the way it got hold of you—it was always different.

Macleod thanked Jona, turned away, and heard the sergeant traipsing after him. As he looked up, he saw Clarissa coming towards him.

'I'll suit up and get a look,' she said, but Macleod could see her hands beginning to shake.

'Don't,' he said. 'Don't. Sit this one out but get the photographs. Go and see Jona's photographer. Get the photographs. The body's the same in that it has these carvings on them. Go wake up your professor.'

'Now?' queried Clarissa. 'It's getting to be the middle of the night.'

'And?' said Macleod. 'You're up. I'm up.' He saw Clarissa raise an eyebrow. 'Sorry,' he said. 'Go and raise her, though, because I don't want to be behind the curve if there's some connection here. It isn't the exact same symbols. There's a difference.'

But that same upside down cross, he thought, *like it's teasing me.* Clarissa nodded and Macleod watched her go and she took a wide berth past the crime scene over towards the forensic wagon.

'You don't have to protect her like that,' said Hope.

'Of course, I do,' said Macleod. 'There's no point dragging her into crime scenes, especially ones like that, if it's going to knock her for six. We need her. We need the way she thinks, the way she punches and goes in at things. You're okay. You can keep your head when you see stuff like that. Me too. Not that it doesn't affect you, but you can keep your head. She won't.'

Macleod could see that Hope wasn't convinced by his argument, but he ignored her and continued back to the flat to see Sandra Mackay, the bereaved mother. As they got to the front door, a constable let them in and he saw inside a woman wrapped up in a dressing gown and a blanket, sobbing on the sofa. Beside her was a family liaison officer he recognised, who stood up and made her way over to him as he approached.

'She's been like this much of the time, Inspector. I'm afraid she might not be much use. She blabbers on about the fact she went out and then she doesn't remember anything.

'I'll talk to her anyway,' said Macleod. 'You never know what might come.'

He strode over and sat down on a sofa opposite, while Hope came to the middle of the room and knelt. Macleod gave a nod and Hope put her hands out to the woman, touching the back of hers.

'Sandra. Mrs Mackay? Sandra?'

'It's Miss.'

'Sorry, Sandra. Miss Mackay. I'm Detective Sergeant Hope McGrath and this is my boss, Detective Inspector . . .'

'I know him. I know you. Seen you on the telly. Guess I can't blame you, can I? Guess I can't. You were not long onto this, were you? There was that other one that died. The other kid. It's on the news, just the same. Did they have those, those . . . ?' She bent over, crying.

Hope reached out with her hand, trying to comfort the woman. When she'd rallied, Macleod got up off his chair and came and knelt in front of her, too.

'Sandra, I'm sorry that this has happened. All I can do is find out who did it, why, and make sure they don't do it to someone else. I can't bring back Britney, but I can stop some other mother feeling like you do, some other father going through this. I need to talk to you, and I need you to do your best to help me identify what happened.'

The woman nodded and then her head went back down again.

'Take me through what happened,' said Macleod. 'Start off with what you did.'

'I left Britney here. Britney's always okay. I was going out in the evening. I had the television on for her, that kid's channel. It goes on to three in the morning. She just falls asleep eventually.'

Macleod couldn't believe what he was hearing; that her mother just simply left a child in the house to go out. She'd paid a price for it, though, and he wasn't about to rip into her.

'You went out. Where did you go and why?'

'I went out for some fun,' said Sandra. 'I went out because you get stuck here. You get stuck here with her every day, every night. I don't like these kids' programs. I have to watch them, and I sit with her and it just drags and no man wants you. You get that, Inspector? No man wants you if you've got a kid like this.'

'Do you take drugs, Sandra?' asked Macleod.

She lifted her head. 'What the hell do you think?'

'Sell them?'

'No. I'm just a mug that buys them. I went out to the club, Bailey Shoes, that one.'

'Just on the edge of town. You go down a back alley to get to it, don't you?' said Hope.

'It's all dance, trance music, rave. It's great. You just drift away.'

'You take anything when you were there?' asked Macleod.

'Several things, I can't remember what they were. Had half a bottle here before I went out just to loosen up. Then I went and danced. I remember I danced.'

'Remember anything else?'

'There was someone there, someone. Some man. Several men, actually, I think. I don't know. Might have been the dealer. He was passing the stuff out; spent the money and danced and then I think I came back here with someone . . . I think.'

'You don't know if you came back and had sex with some-one?' asked Hope.

'That's right. Terrible waste, isn't it? I don't know. Must have been rubbish. Can't even remember him.'

'You were so far gone you couldn't even feel anything,' said Macleod. 'Or maybe he put something into you, some drug. Are you happy if we take some bloods? Might help us trace what happened to you. I think you might have had something a bit more than what you normally have.'

'I didn't get up until seven the next day, seven in the evening. I don't have a problem getting up. Usually, Britney's up and jumping around making noise and I get up too. Little Britney,' she bowed her head again, starting to cry once more.

'Stay with me,' said Macleod. He thought he almost sounded unkind. 'Do you normally pick up men? Is it your standard practice?'

'Yes,' she said. 'Usually, they're here in the morning. I can't say I remember every single one, but I remember. You know?'

'Then that's when you went out to look?'

'You can ask next door. We both ended up looking and that's when I came across her. At the end of the . . .'

The woman bent over, sobbing bitterly again and this time her head didn't come back up. Macleod motioned for the liaison officer to step in and called Hope away.

'What do you make of it?' he asked.

'Some mess. You're going to have to try and get some bloods out of her if she's okay for us to do them.'

'Absolutely,' said Macleod. 'I also would like to know if she's had sex or whether she's just passed out. It's a bit of an invasive check but if she'll agree to it, it might help us with the man. DNA, that sort of thing.'

'What's bothering you, Seoras?' asked Hope.

He motioned at her to go back outside of the flat and he took a nod from the door constable as they did so. Outside in the cool, he whispered quietly to Hope.

'The first murder. You have the child, you have the symbols, and you have a mother who hasn't been touched, who seems to have died accidentally, almost been looked after to a point, just not very well in the execution of keeping her alive. This time she goes out, someone has picked her up, quite possibly fed her something, drugged her in some way. Then she wakes up later and she can't recall if she's had sex but yet . . .'

'You're thinking what?' asked Hope. 'Two people, two different killers? Copycat?'

'Not copycat. No. We locked that scene up tight. There's nothing in the media about symbology, nothing about the children being mutilated, cut. The question is then why does somebody come along? Jona's just said that the symbols, she thinks they're done by a similar blade but she's not sure. They're not the same. We have a mother who the first time isn't interfered with in any way. In fact, it was almost a case of she was going to stay alive except they screwed up.

'Now here, the second case, I think she's actually had sex with someone and if she was that far gone, there was no need to. If they gave her a drug, they put her under till seven in the evening; the only reason you would is because you wanted to. Very, very different from the first scenario. And if the first scenario and the second scenario were so different and it's different people, what worries me, Hope, is that this isn't a serial killer or a copycat killer. What bothers me is that this is

82

something more than that. The symbology, cultish? Some sort of, the word seems wrong, but club? Ritualistic club, society? It's too horrific for words, but what else do you call them?'

'If this starts to get out, we could be in trouble,' said Hope. 'Because if you're a society like that, you've got to ask why they're doing it. Is it for notoriety? If it is, the more it gets out, the more you do. If it's for some God-forsaken cult purposes, if they are somehow satanic or something akin to that, then where's this going to go?'

'I need you to go and track where she was that evening. It's going to be colder now, the trail, because we are what, thirty hours in? She missed a large part of the day. It also makes me think there are two killers here. Just the timing of it.'

'But it's possible that somebody could have done both.'

'It's possible, but that's a bit of a nippy, speedy effort, isn't it? I mean what? You race off from one and run to the other? How were these women picked out? Just randomly? Not in this case. You don't randomly nab Sandra and then come back and think, "Oh, look, there's a kid." What if there wasn't a kid? If the point is to kill the kids, the point is to put these symbols on the kids, you don't go out and just randomly pick a woman.

'They've been watched. I'm sure they've been watched. Notice the victims are all so different. One boy, one girl. With regards to the mums, one's a druggie. Sounds like she's a right mess. Quite possibly sleeps around a lot. The other was your just average mum getting on with things. Massive difference. Serial killer? If it was the same person, I'd be banking that most of the time the target would be similar. You get comfortable, you know how to commit a murder. I'm not convinced this is the same person at all. I'm worried, Hope. I'm very worried. We need to jump on this quickly.'

'Okay, Seoras, I'll get off. You've already told Clarissa to wake up the professor. I'll go and wake up the club, see what I can find. And, Seoras,' she said, putting her hand up on his shoulder. 'We'll get them. We will get them.'

Macleod turned away. He wasn't so sure. *Will we get all of them? How many were there? Was his hypothesis right? Was this some game or club?* He prayed to God it wasn't.

Chapter 11

H ope drove through the Inverness night just as rain began to hit the windscreen of the car. She felt a little chill. It was now three in the morning and the place she was going to would probably be shut. If she was lucky, somebody might be clearing up. As she drove with the tall buildings on either side reaching up in the night like some sort of gothic structure, almost threatening, she felt that chill again.

She didn't know if it was the subject matter of the investigation that was causing her to feel uneasy, but something was. Something was worming a way into her brain. She needed to push back, needed to keep a clear and objective focus. The streets were quiet, little traffic about, but in some way, she wished it was rush hour. The noise of the cars going here and there, of horns blaring, of the occasional screech of brakes would've made her feel more attuned to the city, more attuned to life. Right now, she felt out on the edge.

Hope parked up a little way out of the city centre, finding the back alley that the club entrance lingered in. Linger was the right word, for the outside showed a shabby sign and had two doors that looked better as an emergency exit than the gateway to any sort of paradise. As she approached them, she found them to be shut, but there was light coming through the small crack between the doors.

She thumped on the door hard with her fist and heard a cry of, 'We're shut. Go away.' She banged on it again. There was another cry of, 'Go away,' but this time with a far stronger use of words. Hope continued to thump until the door suddenly sprang open. A man who looked like the side of a fridge appeared, grimacing at her. 'Told you we're shut. Now, go away.'

'My name's Detective Sergeant Hope McGrath. I need to speak to the workforce in here.'

'What for? You need a warrant to come in here.'

'Just calm down, tiger,' said Hope. 'I am not coming in looking for drugs, not coming in looking for anything of that ilk. I'm coming in about a woman who's just lost her daughter tonight. I believe she may have been followed home.'

This wasn't strictly the truth, but Hope wasn't going to go into any detail. 'I need to talk to your staff. It occurred last night, so I'll need you to tell me how many of them were here. I'm on a murder investigation. I know the hour's late, but I really don't need to be held back.'

'I'll just see if the boss is okay with this.'

'The boss is going to be fine with this. Anything else that should draw my attention, you've got two minutes to get the hell out of that building. Am I understood?'

The man nodded, closed the doors behind him. Hope looked down at her watch. She stood tapping her feet and then watched as a half-drunk man came up towards her. He was leery, told her what a good arse she had, before she politely turned around and told him to get out of here before she would tan his backside. He backed away, half stumbling, apologetic, and disappeared up the alleyway, touching both sides repeatedly.

Hope shook her head. How do you get in that state and stay upright? Then again, she'd been like that when she'd been abroad. Somehow, it was okay over there. Not so much here. With this contemplation on life, she glanced down at her watch again. Two minutes was up. She went to pull open the door when the bouncer suddenly burst through.

'The boss will see you now,' he said.

'Thank you for your cooperation,' said Hope. As she walked past, staring up at him, she realised it was an unusual thing for her to do. Most people were at best on a level with her. Very few did she have to look up to. They were also probably lucky they were getting her. Macleod might have just bust in, raided the place. She didn't need to pull them up for anything. What she needed was to know what had happened to Sandra Mackay that night.

Hope walked into the middle of what looked like a sticky floor, before retreating to the edges of it as a man appeared from the back rooms. He held out a hand, announcing himself as Barry and the boss of the place, and Hope could see he was on edge.

'Barry, I'm Detective Sergeant Hope McGrath. I'm on a murder investigation. I am not here to look at any licensing issues, any potential drug issues, anything like that. I'm not interested. What I am interested in is what happened to a certain woman when she came in here last night. To clarify, that's not the night before this morning we're in, but the night before that.'

It took Barry a moment to work this through.

'Have you got enough staff on? Is it the same crew?'

'Yes,' said Barry. 'It will be. I'll pull them out here for you.'

Hope stood while Barry disappeared and began rounding up people. Soon he had seven people looking at Hope. There were a couple of bouncers, one of whom had been on the door talking to her, and there were several bar staff. Quite a few of them were young. She glanced over at a barman. He was too. Maybe that was the way you did it. Maybe your staff had to look that way. It didn't matter. She reached inside her jacket and pulled out a photograph.

'This is Sandra Mackay. She's lost her daughter recently, murdered. She was in this club not during this shift, but the shift before. I need to know if any of you saw her. I need to know who was interacting with her. First off, does anybody remember this woman?'

A barman put his hand up. He had short black hair, quite bushy eyebrows and had a rather sympathetic look to him. He stepped forward, looking over at the boss, who nodded at him.

'You tell the sergeant all she needs to know. Okay? The sergeant has told me they're not looking at anything except this murder. The sergeant wants to know. The sergeant gets to know. That's the deal, sergeant, isn't it?'

Hope nodded. There was something about the community, even the more nefarious side of it, that when things involved a child, they reacted to it. Barry probably thought he was doing the decent thing, but of course, he expected Hope in return not to step in in other ways. Didn't matter. She hadn't time for that.

'What's your name?' asked Hope to the barman.

'John.'

'All right, John. You and I are going to take a walk into the boss's office. You're welcome to join us, Barry, if you want.'

'It's okay. Everything referring to the woman, anything to do with her is fine.' John seemed to nod, and then he led Hope off to Barry's office. He was quite genteel, opening the door for her, letting her sit down before taking up the boss's seat himself.

'Sandra Mackay, do you know her well?'

'Sandy's in here fairly often. She's a right mess, isn't she? She comes in looking for drugs, pills, and that. It's nothing hard. Barry doesn't let them sell anything too hard in here. It's not worth it to him. You can see the ones who are popping pills and that. Sandy comes in for that and then she dances. She also lingers around a lot of the men. I've seen her walk out with men here all the time.'

'She said as much. How was she that evening?'

'Well, she was half cut when she came in, but that's nothing unusual. She drifted around. She must have taken something because she was up dancing, looking like an absolute lunatic. That's what she likes. Likes to sweat it on the floor. She keeps telling me. That's the trouble. They think they're talking to you, but they're not. They're reiterating things. They're saying the same thing over and over again, night after night. It's what I get paid for, though. Put the drink up, listen to what they say. Give a nice word back.'

'What else happened that night? Who were these men? Did you know any of them?'

'Most of them weren't interested in her. She was up and dancing in front of them and this and that. Then a small man walked into the bar. I remember that because he could only have been about five-two, five-three. When he came in, he came over to the bar and ordered. Now, what did he order, because it was different? I'm trying to remember,' said John. 'He ordered a B52. I remember that because one of the girls said to me, Julie, she said, "What the hell's a B52?" Anyway, I had to make it and then he took it, turned around, started scanning the floor and he saw her. Made his way over to Sandy. Sandy at that point would've spoken to anyone.'

'What did he look like?' asked Hope.

'Small, quite a snappy suit. He had dark shades on. Sorry, it's not that easy in here. I mean it's dark. Lot of flashing lights. You don't see people in their true light. Sorry about that. I'd like to be clearer.'

'Hair colour?'

'I don't know. Dark if there was any. I'm not even sure if he was bald. I make the drink, I hand it over. I mean, I just glanced at him. It's dark from one end to the other. Especially at the bar area. It's just not that well lit. Most of the lights are on the dance floor. Most of the lights behind the bar are the neon type. You don't see people in them. Not correctly.'

'What did he do with Sandy?' asked Hope.

'He went up and I saw him dancing with her. Then, let me think. He was with her again. He was with her outside where the toilets are. That might be important.'

'Why?' asked Hope.

The man raised his eyebrows. 'You don't work the drug squad, do you? If she's going to take something openly, it'll be out there.'

'Did she take something openly?'

'I don't know. I have no idea. He may have just . . . well, maybe to make sure she didn't disappear. That's a bit creepy though, isn't it? Sometimes when people are drunk, they don't want to lose track of people because in a room like this, especially if it's bouncing, they'll not find them again, possibly for the night. It's just one of those things.'

'He must have come in past your bouncers though, mustn't he?' said Hope. 'They'd have got a good look at him.'

'Do you know how many people they see?' said John. 'Don't let me stop you. You can ask them but faces, boom, boom, boom, one after another. We usually don't mind anyone unless they're trouble. If they're trouble, they know, but if he was trouble, he wouldn't have got in. They certainly didn't throw him out from in here.'

'What time did he leave with her?'

'Must have been back end of one, maybe.'

'Do you know if he got a taxi or that?'

'I'm in here. I have no idea. What I do remember was thinking she must have been bad because he had his arm under her, helping her out the door.'

'Is that normal?'

'There is no normal for Sandy in that sense. She can get totally paralytic. Some nights she walks in much happier, sometimes she's so spaced out you have to guide her. You're telling me she had a kid?' said John suddenly, as if this fact that only just dawned on him, even though Hope basically told him her daughter had died.

'Yes. She never mentioned her?'

'Not to me. It was all about the dancing. All about getting the high, all about enjoyment. No, she never mentioned her.'

'Anything else you can remember about the guy?'

'Not really, small. Five feet two.'

'Thank you for that,' said Hope and stood up from her chair, turning to the door. It was then she realised that Barry was standing outside with the door only a crack open.

91

'He hasn't said anything he's not meant to,' said Hope. 'But he's been very useful.'

She walked to the door and opened it, seeing Barry fully now. 'Thanks for your help, Barry. Just want to have a word with the bouncers to see if our lady took a taxi or not, if they can remember. Otherwise, that's me. It may come down to it one day. John here may have to identify someone, and I may need a statement about what was going on. From what he's told me tonight, there's nothing there to incriminate you.'

'Well, given the subject matter,' said Barry, 'I think it's the least we could do.'

'The least you could do,' said Hope, 'is don't let people get stoned in here. Don't let the drugs come in the door.' The man looked at her, with a very straight face. 'Whatever you do,' said Hope, 'don't trade them yourself.' She watched for a ripple of emotion but the man said nothing. 'Thank you.'

'This will be the second. Won't it?' said Barry. 'There was that other one down by the river. Have you got a serial nut job on the go?'

'There's certain things you won't tell me, Barry, and that's . . . I understand, it comes with your work. There are certain things I won't tell you, and don't take offence because that comes with my work. Thank you.'

Hope extended a hand and the man shook it. 'Like I say, I'm investigating this murder. That's all I want. John will probably have to come down for a statement.'

'John's entitled to do that and he'll get my backing on it.'

'Good,' said Hope and walked off through the club towards the front doors, which were opened for her by one of the bouncers. His colleague was behind him, stacking up some crates. Both were taller than Hope and certainly wider.

However, they looked slow on their feet.

'I need to ask you a question, guys. It's all right. The boss has okayed it. When Sandra came out,' she held up the photo again, 'she might have gone for a car, a taxi. There was a small man, five-two-ish, helped her out, wearing shades. Either of you remember that?'

They both looked at each other, shaking their heads. 'No, but we see so many people, and to be honest, if they go out that way, you're not paying them any attention. They're coming in, well, then they get the scrutiny because that's our job.'

'Did you see a five-two man in shades then?' asked Hope.

'Possibly. We see so many. Only the ones that give you hassle tend to stick.'

'They said that inside. All right, boys. You have a good evening.'

Hope stepped out of the club into the cool night air. So, he'd walked in, possibly plied her with something, took her out. By the time she got to the house, she'd have been paralytic, but he must have known where the house was. Would she have been in a state to tell him?

She'd been watched; it was planned. *Someone had been spotted by Ian, the man who followed Amanda. He saw a bald, lanky, thin, six-feet-tall man. Ian Lamb himself was smaller than that, five-five and now we've got a five-two person. We've either got some clown who can operate on his knees or his feet, or maybe Seoras is right.* Hope walked off into the night to find her car, the chill slightly stronger than before.

Chapter 12

Clarissa Urquhart was wishing that she had a car that had a better roof. Frankly, she couldn't be bothered putting it up tonight, but the cold was gnawing her skin. Her shawl didn't feel as warm as it normally did, and a sudden shower had left her momentarily soaked before stopping when she'd managed to get the roof up.

She had driven initially to the university, aware, of course, that the professor probably wouldn't be in, but she'd managed to get the night-gate security man to chase somebody up, who then woke up somebody else, before finally getting an address for the professor. It was some distance out of Inverness, deep in the countryside and her eyes strained as she watched the light sweep across the road back and forward as a car sped around the twisty road.

Normally, she liked driving, but at this time of night with the way she felt, having been up previously the night before, the chill was getting to her. It didn't help when she found the cottage; she had to park some way down the drive because there was a locked gate. Clarissa then clambered over the fixture in the most unladylike fashion she could think of and began to traipse up the driveway.

It was gravelly, and she made quite a noise but more than that, it was completely dark until she got right in front of the house, standing before the door when a security light came on. Everything had been dark. Was it just the case she was working on because she felt uneasy, on edge as if someone were watching? Maybe she was just fatigued, maybe she was just . . . or maybe she was just spooked.

She'd been thankful that Seoras had told her not to go and look at the body, but she'd seen the photographs and that was just as bad. *The poor mites, both of them, and their mothers.* People didn't deserve things like that no matter who they were. Now, as the hour approached close to four, she found herself about to awaken a professor who hadn't really taken to her that well in the first place.

She banged hard with the large brass knocker on the door. The clang banging broke the still of the night and a dog some distance away began to bark. When there was no answer, Clarissa thumped again, this time even harder, causing the dog to bark back again. She saw a light go on upstairs and then heard somebody trudge downstairs and the door opened in front of her. In a dim light was the professor; her hair was down onto her shoulders. Clarissa thought it suited her better, giving her less of a fierce look. However, she made up for that with the way her eyes penetrated Clarissa.

'What in the blazes are you doing out here at this time? One was asleep.'

'My deepest apologies but I need you to look at some new symbols.'

'I said I would do the research and I will, but you really shouldn't be pestering one at this time of the night.'

If she said 'one' again, Clarissa thought she would hit her.

One is on a murder investigation; one has had another child die and carved on. One would like you to have a look at said symbols to see if we can get ahead.

'You're telling me this wouldn't wait until the morning.'

'My boss, Detective Inspector Macleod, said I needed to get the symbols to you tonight, soon as, get an analysis in case we get behind the curve on trying to prevent another murder. This is two children that have died. He thinks we might be able to prevent another one by getting there as quickly as possible. We've been working through the night on this but if you want me to go back and tell him that the professor thinks we can wait until the morning, I'll gladly do that, and at approximately,' she looked down at the watch on her wrist, 'forty-five minutes time, he'll be banging this door, and he won't bang it like I have. He'll take the ruddy thing off its hinges and he will ask you why you're delaying his investigation.'

It was very heavy-handed but frankly, Clarissa didn't give a stuff. She was exhausted, she needed this, and she needed it now. If the woman was going to mess her about, she wasn't taking any of it.

'It won't be necessary to bring your inspector, or whatever guff you'll stand here telling me but he needs to know I'm not his little dog on his beck and call.'

Clarissa thought she should change tact. 'Of course not,' said Clarissa more congenially, 'but he wanted the best. He wanted someone who really knew stuff, who he could trust.'

The woman gave a smile for a moment and then she looked at Clarissa, 'He barely knew my name before this case you're on, and he wouldn't have had a clue who I was. In fact, I'm probably the only person within any reasonable distance of Inverness that does know any of this stuff, so one understands one's importance . . . and you'd better come in.'

Clarissa thanked the woman, stepped inside the small cottage, and was directed across to a living room.

'Where are these symbols?' the woman asked, switching on a light. Clarissa took out an envelope and handed it to her. The woman swept some books off a coffee table and started placing the photographs side by side. 'If you pop into the kitchen, there's a kettle, make us both something,' said the woman. 'I'm sure you're cold; one is.'

That wasn't much of a statement, and basically, she told Clarissa to go make the tea, but Clarissa saw it as a victory, some sort of friendship won. They needed Professor Wisecroft, so there was no point in upsetting her.

It took Clarissa some five minutes to find and make the tea. When she came back through, she thought the professor looked at the liquid in the cup as if she had been handed bleach. Clarissa wasn't the best at making the teas and coffees, certainly no Ross, but she did know how to make a decent one.

'I don't know if it's the same killer,' said the professor.

'Why do you say that?' asked Clarissa.

'Look,' the professor said and she pointed to a photograph that Clarissa had handed her. 'The cuts from the other day, they're cleaner. These aren't some different form of symbolism. I can tell you what the symbol is, but it's not drawn well. Yesterday, when you came to me last, well, they were perfect, very, very distinct, very clear. Some of these are varied but again, it's the same thing, Mayan cultures, Norse, some Goths, Egyptians, Romans; from everywhere, all talking about death and talking about crossing over. Again, the upside-down cross right in the middle; maybe that's because that's the one they know best.'

'But you said the upside-down cross was different to the rest. You said that's like an enemy. It's the other side, but the other words are not. They're more just about the passage of death, about where we go with the journey. It's not actually something that's opposed to life. Is that summation correct?' asked Clarissa.

'Exactly, that's why these don't make sense. Not like that. One would have thought it would've been quick for a copycat and I assure you that one has not passed these symbols on to anyone else,' said Professor Wisecroft. 'I would hate you to think that I have been sloppy in handling this material. I've taken it in the strictest confidence and the faculty don't even know I have it.'

'Good,' said Clarissa, almost absentmindedly. 'The thing is that it might be somebody else but not a copycat. The symbology didn't get out. Not from us, not from you. That would point to such a possibility. A group of them may be following a leader, maybe being tasked to do it.'

The professor suddenly looked excited. 'Maybe there'll be more symbols to check. Maybe we'll be able to . . . '

'Stop,' said Clarissa. 'Sorry, but this is not a scientific jolly. These symbols are going on kids. Kids that die, so please.'

'Of course,' said the professor. 'Sorry, I don't do these things. I don't get involved. One is immune to a lot of daily life. The joy of academia.'

Well, I'm not immune to daily life, thought Clarissa. *Not at all.* 'Anything else you can tell us about the symbols or any of the leads?'

'This one here. I've also been working on what you gave me previously. I was going to bring it along, but as your inspector seems to be so keen to have the information here and now, I guess I'll just pull up what I was doing.'

The woman beetled off into the next room before returning with several pieces of paper. 'I can email him with this if you want, but I have prepared a copy for him.'

'You can email it to me,' said Clarissa. 'He'd be lucky if he finds an email in the next week.'

'Well, whoever,' said the professor. 'So, I'll give you the short version. If you look at some of these symbols, they've been traded about for years, linking to all these different cultures, so I thought rather than try and nail down any of the specifics of the cultures and really go in there, given the randomness of the symbols, I thought it better if I look at groups who dealt with these symbols. There are some legitimate ones online. When I searched, I find that some of them are appearing on a flag of a group, and I can't find an address for the group. In fact, I'm not sure quite who or what they are. It was a comment at the bottom of a Facebook post and then they did emojis. That's the term, isn't it? One's never too sure, but these emojis looked like some of the symbols you have here. In fact, I would say that all the emojis are included across our two corpses. I haven't seen all of these symbols being used together anywhere else.'

'There was a Facebook group?'

'Yes, I messaged them to try and see if I could get more information.'

'You did what?' said Clarissa.

'I messaged them. I wanted to see if they knew anything else. Thought that was quite reasonable. They have seen the symbols there.'

'No,' said Clarissa. 'No, no, no, no, no. Last thing you needed to do; you needed to tell us about them. Hold off. Who were they?'

'Dark Union, the Facebook page is up with, I'll show you.' The professor tapped some information into the laptop and the Facebook page came up, except it didn't. It wasn't there, just a message that that group didn't exist.

'It's not there anymore. It was there the other day. I looked it up, I commented on it. Look.'

'We'll go in, we'll find out who that's from, but if these people are involved in this, they'll run as soon as you ask,' said Clarissa. 'Sorry, that's just a really dumb move.' She sat down on the woman's sofa and the professor turned around to look at her.

'I'm sorry, I was trying to investigate for you. I didn't realise that.'

'No, you didn't,' said Clarissa. 'This is what I do. Sorry, I probably should have warned you about that. It's as much my fault as yours.'

'Does this set you back?' asked the woman.

'Who knows?' said Clarissa. 'What were the group called?'

'Dark Union. They called themselves Dark Union, which kind of makes sense, doesn't it? You've got all these different cultures and with death in there, it's just sort of a union, gathering them all together and it certainly is dark. It's not about the more pleasant side of life.'

'No, it's not. Now, I need to get up and go and tell my boss what you've found. I also need to get a friend of mine onto chasing up that internet connection before it goes cold. Don't worry, Professor, you've done well and maybe I'll be back for more. If there's anything else you discover in the meantime, just give me a ring.'

Clarissa stood up and she felt her knee started to give away and she sat back down again.

'Are you okay?' asked the professor.

'No, it's four in the morning and unlike yourself, I have been on the go all day, all of the night, trying to chase up this killer, and now at this tender age, I feel like my legs are starting to give away. I don't do through the night any better than I used to. I was never good at nights. I'm getting worse.'

'Let me help you then. I'll drive you back.'

'I've got my car with me. I'll be fine,' said Clarissa. She walked to the front door of the cottage, opening it, stepping out as the security light came on, and turned to face the professor who had followed. 'I know I'm a bit annoyed and grumpy,' said Clarissa, 'but you've done a good job here. He'll be pleased. Macleod will be pleased.'

'Anytime,' said the professor. 'Anytime.'

Clarissa turned around and started walking away. *Seriously?* she thought. *She actually messaged them. We're running a murder investigation and she messages someone who's showing all the symbols. Academics, all the brains and not an ounce of common sense.*

Chapter 13

Macleod stretched in his chair and threw down the reports from the crime scenes. He wanted a moment to just to turn away, to think about something else entirely. His mind kept racing back to the scenes. The two young children and the mess the killer had made of them. It was okay talking about a professional detachment, but it got to you. It always got to you. You just had to know what to do with it, how to cope, when to seek help when your coping mechanism didn't work.

The door opened and Ross dropped a cup of coffee on his desk, and Macleod gave a brief 'thank you'. He didn't want to talk to Ross at this moment. Indeed, Ross probably didn't want to talk to him. It happened when you came back from crime scenes like this. People were processing, trying to take away that emotional pull and focus on the professionalism that will get them the result they wanted. He reached forward, took the black coffee, sipped it, and found the reassuring taste he was used to.

Beside him, the telephone rang, and he picked it up, pressing it to his ear while he drank another mouthful.

'I hope I didn't wake you.' It was Jane, Macleod's partner.

'I thought you'd probably still be up since you hadn't come home. I take it, it wasn't good news.'

'No, there's been another one.'

'Same as before?'

'Yes, same as before. You really don't want to know.'

'I probably don't. I'm here if you need me; you know that.'

'Always, and when this one is done, if you want to take me on one of those short breaks you organise.'

'You don't usually like the short breaks I take you on.'

'I won't care. I'll need to switch off from this one big time.'

'You think it will be quick?'

'I don't know,' said Macleod. 'I really don't.'

It was as if Jane was waiting to say the next bit, holding back, unsure how he would take it, but then she seemed to just jump in anyway. 'The news is reporting a serial killer, a serial killer of kids.'

'For once the news is probably right.'

Jane became quiet on the other end of the phone. Then, as if the silence was haunting them both, she blurted out, 'Just take care of yourself, okay?'

'I always try to. Don't always succeed.'

'No, you don't. Just make sure you do this time.'

Again, there was an awkward silence until Macleod broke it.

'How have you been anyway? I don't think I've seen you for the last couple of days.'

'The usual. Was down at the pool doing the aquafit. Popped over to Andy's two down round the corner. His mum died, so I took him a little something. You know, keeping busy, like a good detective inspector's wife should while she waits for her man.'

'You wait for your man,' laughed Macleod, but not with his

heart in it. 'You're all right though, aren't you?'

'Of course, I'm all right, Seoras. I'm fine. You going to be home tonight?'

'Don't know. Seriously do not know.'

'Did you get any sleep last night?'

'Maybe two hours in this chair. It was a good job I got them to get me a comfy one.'

'What about the rest of the team?'

'All out and about, as ever,' he said. 'I'm going to have to start thinking about fatigue very soon, though. I could do with a rest but it's all go, given the nature of it.'

'It's all go, all right,' said Jane. 'It's all over the news now. They're starting to come in with it.'

'What are they saying exactly?'

'Well,' said Jane, 'from what I've heard on the radio and seen, two children died; there's a mother died as well. They're talking about some man going around killing them. Says you haven't let any of the press near the crime scenes.'

'We don't let people near the crime scene anyway.' said Macleod. 'They always make that sound so suspicious, like we're trying to hold something back from them.'

'But you are, aren't you?' said Jane.

'Yes, and I'm holding it back from you because you don't need to know about it.' Again, there was a silence.

'Okay.' said Jane. 'I'll let you get on. You need anything, you know where.'

'I'm nearly running out of these shirts. I had a couple spare here, but . . .'

'Do the usual. Leave them in the office whenever. If you're not in, I'll pick them up. I still think you should get this on the tab. They should be paying you for this when you're not going home.'

'I think the case is going to be easier to solve than getting that done.'

There was a little grunt of amusement from Jane, but her tone seemed more serious. 'If you're not telling me, it's bad. Look after yourself. Look after the rest of them.' Macleod was about to say goodbye when there was a knock on his door. Before he could say come in, the DCI marched through the now open door and appeared in front of his desk.

'Anyone important, Macleod?'

'Very!' He was tired. He was going to be irritable, but the man deserved that.

'Sorry, I probably should have waited outside the door.'

'You probably should,' said Macleod, and returned to the phone. 'I'll try and speak to you later, Jane. Not sure if I can, but you know.'

'I know,' she said, and the phone call ended.

Macleod pointed to the round table at the side of his office where the team usually sat together for briefings, indicating that the DCI should sit down. He stood up from behind his desk, gave a stretch and walked out to the front door looking into the office for Ross.

'Any of that coffee left? DCI needs one.'

'DCI doesn't drink coffee,' said Ross. 'DCI drinks tea. Herbal. I think I've got some.'

Macleod nodded, and then turned to the seated man who for some reason didn't drink coffee. The conversation had been quite audible, and the DCI almost apologised.

'Don't like the caffeine in it. Keeps me awake at night.'

'That's why I take it,' said Macleod. He hadn't been long with DCI Lawson and in truth, Macleod did not know the man well.

He was short, possibly five foot three on a good day, but had golden locks and a wad of hair that looked like it needed to be cropped more often. The man was younger than Macleod, maybe by twenty years, and he was good looking as well, but Macleod had long got over those things and he didn't hate the man for that. In fact, he didn't hate the man at all. He was just grumpy and irritable because he was tired.

'I wanted to come in and touch base with you on the case. Obviously, I wanted to do it earlier, but now we've got a second victim.'

'A third,' said Macleod. 'The mother died at the first crime scene as well.'

'Of course,' said Lawson. 'Of course. There's been a lot of press speculation. Child killer, whipping things up.'

'Nothing's come out about the symbology then?' asked Macleod. The man looked up at him quizzically.

'You said they cut into the children. That's what I read. Symbols but . . .'

'Symbols. Lots of symbols, and if the actual symbols get out there, the press will realise that they're all about death. Then a cult picture breeds from it and the press run with it and they scare the wits out of everyone,' said Macleod. 'Just when we really need calm heads, and the message to be careful when you're out and about, especially women with children. Go in groups. Try not to be alone. Each of these attacks on the children didn't happen in the moment; they were planned.'

'Indeed. I can see where you're coming from. I want to start pushing down the Ian Lamb line though,' said the DCI. 'He looks like a very good suspect. Ogling that woman, has an entire flat that he's taken over cutting holes into her bathroom and bedroom. Sounds ideal for this sort of thing.'

Macleod lifted his head, which had sunk down listening to what he seemed to think was a drone from his DCI. He had hoped that the man would come in with a bit of sparkle, give some insight that Macleod was missing, but instead he was ploughing down a line that was so obvious that Macleod was worried about it.

'We've got a problem on that, sir,' said Macleod.

'It's not sir. The name's Alan. Alan Lawson. If we're going to work together, Macleod, we should at least be on first name terms.'

Macleod's head flicked up. 'Then call me Seoras.'

'Some of the others seem to think you like being called Macleod.'

'I think they like calling me Macleod. Don't think they're friends with me because most of them aren't. Quite a lot of them fear me, which is wholly unfair.'

The door was rapped and when Macleod shouted to come in, Ross marched through holding a cup of herbal tea in his hand. He shuffled around the side of the table and placed it down in front of the DCI. 'There you go, sir,' said Ross.

'It's Alan. Please just call me Alan.'

'I will do. I'm Alan as well. Detective Constable Alan Ross.'

'I know, I've read about you. Macleod doesn't want to let you go, does he?'

'The Inspector doesn't, no. We've worked together now for quite a while.'

'Darn right, I don't want to let Ross go. The best man I've got for getting into the computers. Also makes good coffee.'

The DCI stared at Macleod and then back to Ross. 'Like I said, I thought we were on first name terms. Isn't that right, Seoras?'

'Yes, it is, Alan,' Macleod said to the Chief Inspector.

'Well, if that's the case then,' said Ross, not understanding what had gone on before, 'I'll just pop back out to the office, if you need me, sir, won't be a problem.'

'That's fine, Ross. I know where you are.'

Alan Ross stepped out of the office in his rather sombre but convivial mood he came to meet everyone with. Behind him, the DCI stared at Macleod.

'He just called you sir.'

'Yes, he does that.'

'And you call him Ross.'

'Doesn't like first name. He's never Alan. Even amongst the rest of the team, he's not Alan. You've got Clarissa. You've got Hope. They get to call me Seoras. Ross doesn't, won't have it. Calls me sir.'

'You're okay with that?'

'Why wouldn't I be? Goes back to the times we had before. I think he does it out of respect. Either way, it's up to him and he's always been Ross.'

The DCI looked a little bit bemused for a bit but then looked down at some papers he had with him. 'Okay, Seoras, like I say, I want to go down the Ian Lamb line, pull him in properly, make him our main suspect.'

'You can do that, of course, if you want. I understand that this investigation could go up higher to be taken on by a more senior officer, but I would seriously debate bringing Ian Lamb in at all. The man's not a killer. He's an out-and-out pervert and what he did was a gross invasion of privacy. Then he went and slept with her. Amanda Hughes actually slept with the man.'

'It does let us know though how he managed to get close to

her to arrange the killing.'

'For what reason? And with all the symbology, there's nothing to indicate that he's involved in anything occultic or even belongs to any particularly weird groups. When I say that, I mean groups involved in esoteric matters. I think he's someone that needs serious help.'

'Well, I'm telling you to go down that line.'

'Why?' asked Macleod, suddenly. He was going to be gentle. He was going to explain once over again why Ian Lamb was not a good suspect, but he was tired, and he was fed up. There was little enough breaking in the case without having to charge down the wrong line because they didn't have anything.

'Well, whoever it is came to Sandra Mackay, found her in the club, went back with her and apparently made love to her.'

'So I've heard,' said Macleod. 'I'm waiting on Jona to come back with DNA that they left behind. We need to hold off until that information comes back.'

'Better we take the line, bring him in.'

'No,' said Macleod. 'Unless you make this a specific order, I'm not doing it. I don't think he is a killer.'

'Better to be careful though, isn't it?'

Macleod sat up straight in the chair. 'Careful? You don't think we're careful? You don't think that we think about the consequences of what we do?'

'I'm not saying that.'

'You just have,' said Macleod. 'I'm not convinced, Alan, that that's a good line.'

'Okay, I can see this is gnawing at you. We'll revisit it, though. Get me a hold of something else. Get me some path, something I can keep the savages away from us with.'

'I'll do my best,' said Macleod.

Macleod rose to escort the man from his office, and he could feel the frostiness between them already. It wasn't a good time to pop in. Some of the other DCIs had been better at knowing when to leave him alone, but he guessed the man didn't know that yet. He shouldn't take it personally. Macleod eased himself back behind his own desk, bending his knees with a crack as he sat down. His joints were not good these days. His mobile went and he picked it up, fielding a phone call from Hope.

'I'm just popping home for a shower, Seoras, but I thought to let you know. Different sized man.'

'It's seven a.m. I've been up all night, Hope. Clarify for me?'

'Different sized man, Seoras. The man who took Sandra Mackay home was shorter. I think we're looking at two different people.'

'That ties with what Jona is saying about the cuts, and yet they're still all the same symbols,' said Macleod. 'Go get your shower and then come back. Wish you could get me a change of clothes while you're there.'

'I don't think you'd suit what I wear. Besides, I'm too tall for you.'

Macleod laughed, although it was obviously very forced. 'DCI wants me to pull in Ian Lamb.'

'Unwise,' said Hope. 'You could bring that man in. He'd be the focus of the media, and then we'd never even get round to charging him. Not a good plan.'

'No, it's not, but it's starting, Hope. The pressure for results, the pressure for doing something.'

'So, what are you going to do?'

'I'm going to let my hound away, get Clarissa to get on top of Ross about these symbols and these groups. If it's different

110

killers, and the commonality is the symbols, they're not being generated by the killer. They're being generated by someone else, if you're right about multiple killers.'

She murmured her approval and told him to try to get some rest before switching off her phone. Macleod thought that was the funniest comment of all. 'Get some rest.' He turned and looked out of the window behind him, out into the awakening Inverness. People would be starting to get scared. Two murders. Two murders in quick succession. He felt his hands shake as much from frustration as anything else because he could feel another one was coming.

Chapter 14

'So where are we going?' asked Clarissa, throwing her shawl around her as Ross walked out of the office. It was late in the morning, but he had let her get an hour or two of sleep, albeit in a chair, her head tipped back and snoring loudly. She had been out most of the night with the professor, and then she'd come back with information, giving names of groups and some other sketchy information about the symbols. Ross had phoned people he'd used on a previous occasion. He knew his limits on a computer, his limits on searches, what he could go into and find, especially with the investigation running as well. He would be shuffling bits of paper here and there, making sure everything was dotted and crossed. Invariably, the time to do a truly deep internet search and find all these names would be lost on him. For this reason, he'd picked up the phone and called in some people Macleod probably would've called geeks. Techies, the polite term.

'You've got your car keys?' asked Ross.

'I don't think I'm fit for driving.'

'I'll drive then,' said Ross.

Clarissa stared at him. 'No. Not my car, you don't. I'll keep the hood down. We'll be fine. Air will keep me awake.'

Two minutes later, the pair were spinning out of the Inverness Station's car park in the small green sports car that Clarissa so loved. Ross indicated a right straight out of the car park, heading off towards the industrial estate on the edge of town. Among the large warehouses, there was a smaller section of units with only a few varied companies there, each one operating on a low level. But the one he was taking her to didn't need vast office space or storage space because everything was done from a small hub of computers.

As Clarissa parked the car, Ross stepped out and told her to follow him up to a rather bland, brown front door. As he approached, he looked up to see the CCTV looking down and a voice said, 'Hello, Alan Ross.' The door then swung open on its own and Clarissa followed Ross through into a rather drab corridor. He passed up it, took a left through another rather boring door, and into a room filled with desks and screens.

'Mr Ross, I think we've got something for you.'

Clarissa looked at the man speaking. He had a beard and glasses and yet he couldn't have been over the age of twenty-seven. Clarissa thought that look went out with the seventies. Another young man was clean-shaven, but she noticed a number of items on his desk. Gimmicks, possibly, or were they just characters from different films, those modern films she didn't tend to watch? Superheroes, was it?

Clarissa shook her head but followed Ross as he made for the man who gave them the original greeting. Alan reached forward and put a hand out towards the man as he looked at Clarissa.

'This is Isaac. Isaac Matthews. He does with a computer what I can't do. Isaac, this is Detective Sergeant Clarissa Urquhart. She's pretty au fait with technology and that, but you might have to occasionally say to her what you're doing.'

Clarissa stepped forward, put her hand out to the man, who took it and she shook it, firmly. She bent forward. 'Actually, you might have to tell me a lot of what you're doing because Alan's being very polite.'

The man laughed, then clapped his hands as he released hers. 'Let's settle in then, shall we? Tommy, get these two a coffee.'

Chairs on wheels were provided and Ross and Clarissa sat at the shoulders of Isaac as he brought up different screens in front of him. Clarissa thought she was at some sort of cinema because there were five screens in front, each as big as her single screen in the office. He seemed to fire between one and the other at a speed she was struggling to keep up with.

'I've gone into the chat rooms on the dark web, ones you don't normally see. Lots of other communications and tried to hack into a few other things, ran a simple check with many pictures. Well, it's not been easy. I also tried to look into Dark Union. There's a wide range of groups, and I narrowed it to the occult, talking about things such as sacrifice, child sacrifice, and that. But always with a group feel about it. There's been some chatter about the incidents themselves, but it's generally coming from people on the outside. As far as I can tell, nobody's claiming to have done any of this. There's certainly not been any pictures put up over the incidents yet.'

'Well, that's good to know,' said Clarissa. Her own mind was taken back to the one situation she had seen and then the photographs of the other. 'That's probably lucky, Isaac,' she said. 'It wasn't a pretty sight.'

'What else you got, Isaac?' asked Ross.

'Of the numerous groups, there's only a few with such a wide use of symbols. There's some that relate distinctly to Mayan or Aztec cultures in their groups, others about Norwegian, obviously to do with Norse. Certainly, there are some satanic groups out there as well, but to have all of those symbols involved, there's only a couple of groups. Dark Union, I can't get a firm hit on. It's mentioned very, very rarely, but I do have some people who might be worth looking at.'

'Really?' said Clarissa. 'Like who?'

'Probably the one that's coming up the most is Dr Samuel Forbes. I have an address for him in Inverness. As far as I can tell, he is a medical doctor, but he seems to have an interest in the occult. When I say occult, I mean occult from everywhere. Everything from Lovecraft through to the Mayans and the Satanists.'

'Lovecraft?' asked Clarissa.

'Yes. The works and mythology of H. P. Lovecraft. I say mythology but that's not actually accurate. He made up a whole world himself about elder beings from afar. Some people take it as true because he mixed their culture into ours. He came up with rather convincing stories in that sense. Of course, it's all bumf, but some of these groups don't seem to be able to identify the real mythology, so to speak, from the made-up stuff.'

'Why Dr Forbes?' asked Ross.

'Basically because of the symbols. He's used all these symbols. He's spoken about them. He's in a group that I can't get a link onto at the moment. So, the idea of Dark Union being someone but I don't know who they are fits. He's local, and he is quite high up.'

'High up?' queried Clarissa. 'How do you mean?'

'Top surgeon at the hospital as far as I can gather.'

'That's important how?' asked Clarissa.

'Well, you know, rich people. These sorts of groups tend to be funded by rich people.'

'You're not thinking about the crime scene then?' said Clarissa.

'Isaac doesn't know about the crime scene,' said Ross. 'Isaac works for me. He does a great job but there's certain details he does not need to know. I told him about the symbols, not where the symbols came from.'

'That's pretty normal,' said Isaac. 'I don't need to know. I don't want to know darker, nasty things like that. I will see if I read about them or I see them online, I let Mr Ross know and he can then follow up as he best sees fit, but I'm working a little bit on the outside for him.'

'So, we need to go and see Mr Forbes,' said Clarissa.

'Dr Forbes,' said Ross. 'I've done my bit. Time for you to step up.'

She flicked her head round, saw the cheeky grin on his face. 'Just watch and learn,' she said, 'Just watch and learn.'

* * *

Before setting out for Dr Forbes's house, Ross placed a call to the hospital making sure the doctor wasn't there. It was his day off, apparently, and so the green sports car raced across Inverness again to a plush house on the outskirts, beyond the river. They were almost out in the countryside by the time the house came along. Clarissa turned up a driveway big enough for a lorry, never mind a car. She parked up in front of a BMW, with a Porsche beyond it, and gave a quick look to Ross.

'That's a lack of taste, that's just money. What you're in is a car with essential essence, a car that is alive.'

Ross stared at her. 'I'm in a car without a roof, messes my hair up.'

Clarissa shook her head, told him to get out and clambered out of the car herself. They walked across crunching stones up to a large door which was mainly made of glass. However, the curtains behind it stopped them from seeing into whatever lay beyond. Clarissa looked left and right at the front of the house. It was a new build and she thought it to be rather massive.

'I bet you they live here, the two of them, no kids. You can fit a family of about a hundred and fifty in here.'

The door opened and there was a maid looking at them as if somebody appearing at the door was an occurrence that never happened.

'Hello,' said the maid.

'Hi,' said Clarissa, taking a friendly tone, 'I'm Detective Sergeant Clarissa Urquhart. This is Detective Constable Alan Ross. This is my warrant card and I'd like to see Dr Samuel Forbes if he's in, please.'

The woman lifted the warrant card, staring at it closely before handing it back. 'By all means.' She went to turn but Clarissa called her. 'Do you mind if we wait inside? A little bit parky out here.'

The woman looked as if the question had never been asked and she wasn't sure whether they should be inside or not, so Clarissa took it upon herself and marched into the hallway.

'We'll wait here, it's not a problem. You just go and get Dr Forbes for us.'

There was a slight commotion upstairs before a man came walking down in a smart white shirt with some pale grey trousers. There might have been a tie once, but the shirt was open at the top, and perched on his nose were some small round spectacles.

'Hello,' he said. 'Can I help you?'

'Are you Dr Samuel Forbes?' asked Clarissa.

'Mr Samuel Forbes. The doctorate is from the PhD; I don't use it since I've got my consultancy.'

'Great,' said Clarissa. She looked unimpressed and the man scowled at her. 'I'm Detective Sergeant Clarissa Urquhart. I'd like to ask you some questions.'

'Questions about what?' the man asked.

'Questions regarding some symbols we've had the cause to look at during an investigation. I was wondering if you knew anything about them.'

'Well, if you'd let me have a look,' said the man.

'I'm sure there's somewhere more comfortable than this we can go. Perhaps a library or something would be suitable. Don't wish to disturb your living areas, maybe your wife if she's here.' Clarissa quickly scanned around. 'Is that your study in there, sir?'

'It is, indeed,' said the man.

'Let's go in there then. It's out of the way, keeps us out of the main body of the house, eh? Office time.'

Clarissa didn't wait for an answer but marched off, leaving Ross rather bemused and embarrassed. He shrugged his shoulders as the man looked at him. Samuel Forbes shook his head in a somewhat angry fashion and marched down the hall after Clarissa.

Inside the study of Dr Samuel Forbes, Clarissa found walls and walls of books. Without looking back at the doctor, she marched over and started scanning the titles. The shelf she looked at first had lots of books about medical issues that she thought was pretty normal considering he was a doctor or a consultant or whatever you called them. She then spun over to look at another wall and recognised books about mythology. They were everywhere.

'I see you could be the man we need to talk to.'

'Why is that?' snapped the man.

'Because of these. You know all about mythology, you know all about symbols, probably. Here.' Clarissa suddenly pulled an envelope out from underneath her shawl. Several photographs were extracted and slapped down on a desk in front of him. 'Don't speak about this to anyone else outside of here. Rather disturbing, some of these images, I'm sure.'

'Why should it be disturbing?' asked the man. Clarissa was taken aback for a moment. He was a doctor or a consultant or whatever you called it. Surely, he had to realise those symbols were on a body.

'Do you recognise any of those symbols?' asked Clarissa.

'None,' he said quickly.

'You're telling me you've read all of this stuff and not one of these appears in there?' said Clarissa.

'I'm a medical doctor, not some sort of mad wizard,' said the man. 'I really don't see why you're here talking to me.'

'Have you ever heard of the group Dark Union?' asked Clarissa.

'No,' said the man, 'never. Should I?'

Clarissa stared him in the eye. *That wasn't right,* she thought. It wasn't right. He slowed down, slowed down his comment, thinking, *Should I admit to it or not?* Of course, she had no proof of that, but that was her gut, that was her feeling.

'What are we doing in here?' said another voice. A tall woman entered the room, and the study suddenly became packed. There was barely enough room for two people to stand in front of the desk admiring the shelves of books, but now there were four and everything was being done face to face.

'Samuel, who are these people? Why are they in here? I hope you haven't let them push you into looking at your books.'

'These are police officers.'

'Detective Sergeant Clarissa Urquhart, and this is Detective Constable Alan Ross. Just here to ask your husband some questions. Some books he's got, doesn't he?'

'The fact that my husband is into mythology and medical studies as befits his job does not give you the right to march into our house.'

'Didn't march in,' said Clarissa. 'If you're worried about frightening me with a décor, I've seen worse.'

The woman began to rage as Clarissa stepped forward up to the shelves, scanning the books.

'What are you doing?' asked the man.

'Just seeing if you've got some sort of symbology or something, something that we could look at these photographs with.'

As she turned back, she saw Mr Forbes's wife looking closely at the photographs. Again, there was no shock. It seemed to Clarissa the fact these symbols were on a body was pretty obvious.

'I'll have to ask you to leave.'

'Why?' asked Clarissa.

'We value our privacy and you've just marched in here.'

'Invited. Your husband said it was okay. Why do you need to hide anyway?' asked Clarissa.

The woman's face got even redder. Meanwhile, Alan Ross was standing, carefully taking in everything that was going on around him. He'd said nothing and was amazed at the show Clarissa was putting on.

'You might have heard of my boss,' said Clarissa. 'We're out here doing this for him. Detective Inspector Macleod.'

The name rang a bell, obviously, for both Mr Forbes and his wife reared back slightly. 'I'm out here rather than sending him out because frankly, he's not like me. He'd tear this place down, seize every book in it. Very thorough, DI Macleod, very thorough. Taught Alan here everything he knows.'

'I'm afraid I'm going to have to ask you to leave,' said the wife. 'Otherwise, I'll be . . .'

'What? Forced to call the police?' said Clarissa, almost laughing. 'You could call my boss, but like I said . . .'

'I shall call my lawyer.'

'Very good. I think Alan's done anyway, aren't you?' The pair had turned back to him as Constable Ross simply gave a nod.

'What was he doing?' Samuel Forbes blurted out.

'Observing,' said Clarissa. 'It's what we do ninety percent of the time.'

'Well, you can observe somewhere else,' said the woman, and put a set of hands onto Clarissa to start pushing her out of the room. Clarissa reached forward, grabbing the woman's wrist, and then slowly removed the arms from her body.

'That's enough,' she said. 'That is enough.'

Once outside and back in the sports car pulling away, Clarissa turned to Ross. 'Well, what'd you think? I take it you checked them all.'

'Mayan, Norse, Satanic, Aztec, all the symbologies are there, right down to the last one. He certainly would have the knowledge to carve those symbols.'

'He's a surgeon. He wouldn't have a problem cutting them.'

'Next time, however,' said Ross, 'maybe we could go in my way.'

'I drove the car, I get to decide. Besides, it's Detective Sergeant Clarissa Urquhart, not Detective Constable.'

Chapter 15

Hope McGrath drove her car down towards the local sports centre, making her way through the heavy afternoon traffic. Ross and Clarissa had been out when the sports centre found a bloody knife inside one of their lockers, opened when a particular section had been cleared. It was not going to be in use for the rest of the day, and yet some of the keys were still missing. It was standard practice to simply open the locker and clear it, taking anything inside, and placing it into the lost property goods. However, having found the bloody knife inside, they'd phoned the police who had passed it instantly onto Macleod's team, understanding that they were looking for a knife as a possible murder weapon.

Hope rounded the corner, drove into the car park of the sports centre, and found a space. The area was busy although sooner or later, everyone would start to make that teatime rush home before settling down for the night. Even the sports centres not to be open as late as they used to be these days. Hope sometimes wondered why. She was used to coming out at ridiculous hours to put in her gym work, having got pulled here and there by a case. Then again, life was different for those that worked at nine to five or something like that. It was much more regimented. One issue she didn't have.

Even her partner, John, manager of a car-hire firm, worked a shift roster of sorts. Sometimes she wished she worked regular hours. Sometimes she wished that certain days in the week could be available for doing a certain hobby. She tried to think what hobby she had other than keeping fit. She didn't seem to have one at all. Keeping fit and John, that was it. It was with a touch of sadness, but she walked across to the sports centre pondering if she could fit more into her life.

The manager of the sports centre had hived off the facility into certain sections, managing to keep the swimming pool operating while closing his squash courts and a few other dance halls. The lockers were located beyond the dance halls. As Hope approached, she saw a couple of constables making sure no one entered the scene. Beyond them, she saw Jona Nakamura fitted out as usual in her white coverall, and Hope looked around to see where she could pick one up from. There was a box sitting on the floor someway down the corridor, and as she showed her warrant card to the two constables on duty, she slipped off her leather jacket, ready to put on the coverall.

'Down here,' said Jona. 'Quick. Come on, I'm about to move it.'

Hope slid into the coverall, zipped it up, took the shoe covers, and slipped them over her boots. She didn't run though because she never liked running in these covers. The plastic sometimes slipped under your feet, but she strode quickly to find the smaller woman staring at the inside of a locker.

'Is it one of ours?' asked Hope, staring at a blade.

'I think so,' said Jona. 'You need to orientate with the marks on the body. Look at the curve, similar to what we've already seen on the cuts. I think this could be it or at least one of them.'

'One of them?' queried Hope.

'If we're running on the basis there's different killers, who knows how many knives we've got out there? It could even be a set. I'm not that well up on weaponry in the sense of torture or delicate weaponry. Sure, we can look through ballistic reports in that, but this is different. This is a knife with meaning. Symbols on it there as well. I think you might need to get Clarissa to have a look at this. Might need to go to the art world side.'

'Or the lunatic fringe side. Might be some sort of cult knife. Have you got anything from the locker at all?' she asked Jona.

'There's no prints. The key is gone. Maybe that had prints on it. Probably unlikely but you'd look a bit off standing here with gloves on.'

'Fair enough.'

Jona stepped forward, bag in her hand, picked up the knife with her gloves on, and slipped it in, writing on the evidence bag exactly what was inside.

'There's numerous photographs,' she said. 'You might want to go and talk to the sports centre manager. I'm going to get off and see if there's any results coming through from the DNA checks. I'll give you a ring if there is.'

'Thank you,' said Hope and turned away and walked back up the corridor before unzipping the coverall. She was glad to get out of it. She always felt they were warm, making her sweat. With the height she had, she always felt like some gigantic snowman.

With her jacket restored, she walked to the offices of the sports centre announcing herself and showing a warrant card before being directed into the main office of the sports centre manager.

The office had a number of sports trophies on the wall. A few pictures of the sports manager with various celebrities, all smiling, and looking like they were at some sort of pro-am in a golf tournament. The number of Pringle sweaters and polo shirts was amazing. As she sat down, a rather convivial man stepped out from behind his desk and shook her hand.

'Andy Crossing, Detective. I'm here for you, so ask away what you want to know. I'm feeling a bit of a shock.'

'I'm sure it has been, Andy. What I'd like to know is, do you have any CCTV here?'

'We do have some at the front desk that mainly protects the staff. We don't have any in the changing rooms obviously or along any of the other corridors. Never really needed it to be honest.'

'Does everybody have to come in through that door?'

'Strictly, you're meant to, but if you wanted, you could pop in any of the fire exits. They're not alarmed, and to be honest, people use them all the time to pop out quickly. It's just if you go over to the west side from here, it cuts off quite a walk round from the road into the estate behind us, so I'm afraid that's not really a regimented route in through the front door.'

Blast it, thought Hope, but she smiled politely at the man.

'I'll need to take what CCTV you have. I take it the car park's got something on it.'

'Indeed, it has, and by all means, take what you want. I'll get one of the staff to help you with that. Anything else you'd like to know?'

'Not really sure,' said Hope. 'I need to interview the staff, see if anybody noticed anyone with a knife.'

'I have already asked them,' said Andy, 'and they haven't said so.'

'The ones that opened the locker up, is that standard practice for you?'

'Yes, yes, if a locker has not got the key in it at the end of a session or when the area has been cleared, we open them all up and pop whatever is there in the lost property. If it hadn't been a bloody knife, we'd probably just have cleared it. Given it had blood on it and given that it was quite fancy, as well as what we heard in the press about what's going on with those poor children, we thought we should contact you first.'

'That was very wise,' said Hope. 'How many people do you get through here in a day?'

'People through? Oh, that's a tough one. I'd say we'd get at least one to two thousand, just depending on the day. Bad weather makes a difference.'

'Do you have a record of everybody who uses the facility?'

'There's a facility to pay by cash if you want, but most of our users are on the membership scheme, so by all means, you can have a look through our members.'

'Thank you,' said Hope. 'Let's do that now. Do you have access?'

'Just a moment.' He turned around to the computer at the side of his desk, typed in what Hope thought was a password, and then called her round to start looking at the screen. 'If you'll take a look, Detective, it all gets broken down here into different types of membership. Is there anybody in particular you wanted me to look at because I've got a couple of thousand people here?'

'I want you to look up Ian Lamb.'

'It doesn't ring a bell with me, but like I said, a couple of thousand people.'

The man typed Ian Lamb's name into the computer and it

returned a positive result. 'Do you have any idea of what that Ian Lamb looks like?' asked Hope.

The man pressed a button, and an image came up showing an Ian Lamb that did indeed live downstairs from Amanda Hughes.

'Do you think you could tell me what Mr Lamb was doing over the last couple of days?'

'Well, from what I can see, he is popped in to go for a swim.'

'So, he's definitely going for a swim?'

'Whoa. Not definitely. When you come in and you put your card in, there's a self-service machine that you can say what you want to do. It also works to help with bookings and things, but you go in, you tap your card, and then that's it. Normally, the staff are just watching to see you tap the card. They're not bothering what you go to do. His says he went swimming. I have no idea if he did go swimming. You could certainly try the staff, see if they remembered him, but there's a lot of people going through the pool.'

'I will check because I want to see if he's been here. Also, I want to see if he's been to the front door. The other thing is,' said Hope, 'I guess I can't check if he actually took that key—if he actually used that locker.'

'No, it's very old-style with the lockers. Put your pound in, turn the key, take the key away with you. The locker stays locked until you come back and unlock it with the key. It's not like getting your phone back. There's no facial recognition, nothing like that. Cost too much.'

'I get that,' said Hope. 'I do understand.'

Hope spent the rest of the afternoon interviewing the staff and found that they did indeed remember Ian popping in for a swim. However, she was unable to trace Ian Lamb's movements throughout the sports centre. On the CCTV, he did appear onscreen coming in, and he had a bag with him, before tapping his card, and disappearing off to the swimming pool. When he came out of the swimming pool, he left the entrance area and went into the other part of the leisure centre. The trouble was then, Ian could have gone anywhere else. There was also a cafe up there. She was advised it wasn't uncommon for people to go for a swim, then come out, and have a drink.

She wasn't any further on, and despite the manager's and staff's help, Hope couldn't pin down the actions of Ian Lamb that day and had no way to tie him into the locker, and therefore, the knife.

'Well, you've been a great help,' she said to the sports centre manager, shaking his hand on the way out. She stepped out into the pouring rain, flipped up her collar on her leather jacket, and walked quite slowly towards the car. She was thinking hard about what was going on.

Why would people be doing this? It just seemed so random. It seemed very random for Ian Lamb. Amanda Hughes, yes, he had a connection to her, a very strong connection. He was obsessed with her. Carried out some actions that were not good.

In one of the cases, Hope wondered why he would have wanted to carve these symbols into a child? The symbolism was erratic, jumbled. Was it a cover-up? Was it really something? Either way, the one thing she knew was they were struggling to get this investigation going, struggling to have a piece of flesh to sink their claw into. Sure, they go over the footage again of the CCTV, they could check everywhere, but whoever was doing this, whoever they were, if McGrath's suspicions were to be believed, they also seemed quite good at

129

hiding away. Good at making a clean murder.

Her mobile phone began to ring, and she picked it up, seeing Jona's face.

'Hey, said Jona, 'got a DNA check back. It appears the only DNA traces on the knife we have are of Britney. No other person's DNA is present.'

'It could have been put in there by anybody.'

'Exactly. More than that, it's been cleaned. I'd expect to maybe find a bit of DNA of people who had been using that locker previously but can't at the moment. Seems very bizarre.'

'Ian Lamb is a sports centre member, and he was there,' said Hope. 'I can't tie him down to where he went in the centre and whether he left a knife.'

'Are you thinking what I'm thinking?' asked Jona.

'If your thoughts are, "Why on earth would you take this knife and leave it in a locker to be found?", yes, then you're thinking what I'm thinking.'

'This doesn't make sense.'

'No, it simply doesn't. Anyway, I've got to get back. See if I can bring any more information?'

Hope thanked Jona before getting into the car and preparing to drive off. So far, they had nothing. Everywhere they went were dead ends. Ian Lamb looked like a dead end. Certainly, it looked like only circumstantial evidence against him, and that, as Seoras was always reminding her, was never enough. Couple that with Seoras's feeling about the man, it made her find it very difficult to believe he was a killer.

Chapter 16

S he tried to move her arm, but it didn't seem to be responding. As her head tilted sideways, she could see it, but in truth, the fingers were blurred and as much as she wanted to move them, she couldn't. On her face, she felt something wet. It was like the blast from one of those garden plant sprays. The water vapour drifting across your face, letting you know there's water there but not giving it in any amount that would be useful for anything.

Something dug into her shoulder blade. She tried to wiggle, but that didn't do any good. It felt sharpish, but not like a knife, like the corner of a curb. Large and thrusting, it drove up where her shoulder blade should have been flat. It seemed to be up at an angle, allowing whatever this was to sit in under the blade. She tried to roll her head, got up to the middle point, her eyes focusing up on something grey above before her head collapsed back down, landing on the shoulder it had previously been on, staring again at the outstretched fingers.

She felt like she needed a jump-start from a car or maybe those defibrillator machines, one to come along and wake her up in a stark fashion. Again, she rolled her head up, but this time with an extra effort, and it fell on the other side. There were no fingers to see over there, but in the distance, she could see that there was . . . was it sky or was it just some opening? Where on earth was she? Her back was cold, but that was the only part of her she could really feel now, other than the light moisture landing on her skin. Where on earth was she?

Alice, she thought. *My name's Alice, Alice.* . . . Again, the brain seemed to be struggling basic recall. *France. That's it*, she thought. *Alice France. Where was I? I wasn't out last night, was I? No, she thought, I wasn't.*

Her hand seemed to close tightly all over a sudden. She rolled her head back over to look at it. It was now gripped tight, but then she sprang it open, feeling her body for once, and then there they were. Legs. She had legs. She tried to stretch out. One gave a sharp shooting pain up it. Maybe she'd just been in this position for too long, wherever she was.

She began to feel her other arm coming back to life. Soon both arms were moving, so much so that she put the flat of her hands down and tried to spin herself over onto her front. She couldn't. Whether it was a lack of coordination or a lack of strength on her part, she didn't know. She didn't know how much effort she was putting in. This feeling was bizarre. Was she still dreaming?

Alice tried to channel her thoughts as to what she would do and then brought her arms inside so that they both sat beside her hips. She pushed down. This time she felt her shoulder blade rise up from whatever had been bugging it until she got into an upright position. Then she bent slightly further. For a moment she thought she was going to tipple topple forward, but she didn't. Instead, she remained in this bent curve. Where was she?

She could hear cars. Where were they coming from?

Because they were loud. It was like someone had put her and them inside a box where the noise reverberated off the walls, consistently. She shook her head. Where had she been?

That was right. It was a swimming pool. She'd been to the swimming pool and there'd been a man. There'd been a man there watching. It was the mums and toddlers' group. She'd been in with Sarah. It had been a weekly session. She'd taken her into the pool, and she remembered someone was watching them. Someone had been looking down. It was a man.

Alice had felt quite strange about it because he was looking at her. He wore a beanie hat and had a beard, a large beard. She thought he looked like one of those strict Jews, the beard was so big, but he didn't have one of their caps. Instead, he had a beanie hat and he looked at her. He had *stared* at her. She had felt uncomfortable and turned her back. Turned away with Sarah in her arms, making the child go splish-splash in the water, the young legs going out, then in, out, then in.

He'd been there for most of the session they'd had. Even though Alice must had turned her back on him, she kept checking. Sure enough, he hadn't moved. When they'd got out, she had gone up to the cafe, which had the observation deck where the man had been, but he was long gone. What had happened then?

She felt a sudden burp, an eruption of wind up through her mouth. Then her stomach pulled in tight before it led out a little roar.

I'm starving, she thought, *I'm starving. We'd gone home. We'd gone home and we'd got out from the car and then . . .*

Suddenly, fright overtook her as she remembered he, or somebody, had grabbed her. Somebody, as she'd got out at her house from the car, had grabbed her. They'd put something over her mouth, and she'd blacked out. They were gone. That must mean that Sarah was still in the car. She needed to get back to Sarah, needed to find out where she was. She rolled over on her hip and then to her knees, trying to raise herself. Her eyes saw only concrete around her. The car noises were behind her, or were they reverberating off what was above?

She looked up, and saw more concrete. It dawned on her; she was on the underside of a flyover. *Tucked up high and away from prying eyes*, she thought. She looked left and yes, there was daylight out that way. Then she looked right. The shock of what Alice saw forced her hands to lose their strength and she crashed down face-first into the concrete in front of her.

She fought to get back up and look again. She saw a little figure lying on the ground, the shirt ripped off its back. On the back were numerous symbols carved into the flesh. Alice didn't want to, but she reached forward and turned the little head, realising it was Sarah.

She'd known. She'd known straight away. She didn't have to be told, didn't have to see, but the horror from looking coursed through her. She tried to stand up, hit her head on the concrete roof, realising how narrow the area was she was in, and instead reached forward and grabbed the child.

She held her close and then began to slide down the large concrete interior, down to the road. As she reached the bottom, she tried to stand up on her feet, wobbling, tears now streaming down her face, panic-stricken. Without thinking, she crashed onto the road and a car blared its horn and screamed with its brakes as it slid past her. Another one did the same. Then the traffic came to a halt on this side of the road, one by one, each car stopping.

A driver got out, shouting at her, telling her, 'Crazy woman.'

Another one got out and looked at her, asking how she was. Alice turned to him, holding Sarah, told him, 'Ambulance.' The man took one look at the bloody child and ran. From further back, someone ran up shouting they were a doctor, shouting that they could help. Sarah looked, sought for the voice.

Everything seemed to ring unclear. Everything seemed to swing about. Her legs felt like they would go from under her. She stumbled forward before flopping onto the bonnet of a car. Her head looked up. She saw an elderly couple, frightened. Then an arm touched her shoulder.

'Dr Menzi. What's the matter?'

Alice couldn't even speak. Instead, she rolled onto her back, holding Sarah in front of her.

'Dear God,' said to the doctor. 'Dear God. We need to get her in hospital now. Come on.'

He shouted over at someone else, and Sarah found arms being shoved underneath her shoulders, almost picking her up off the ground. She looked around. Where was Sarah? *I need Sarah*, she thought, tears rolling down now, streaming in a flood. Everywhere she looked was blurred, but she didn't know if it was from the tiredness or just from whatever drug or malady that was causing her lack of strength.

She felt herself being thrown into the back of a car and some woman was sitting beside her holding Sarah. She reached over to grab her back. That was her Sarah, nobody else's. She'd say what happened to her?

She grabbed her back and at once felt the cold of the child. She didn't know what to do. The car was now driving fast. Maybe she should get out, keep Sarah safe. She opened the door producing shouts from the man driving. Someone reached across her, pulled the door shut. Her head leaned backwards, up where the headrest was missing.

What's going on? she thought. *What's going on? It had been him, hadn't it? It had been him at the house, surely.*

The car stopped. The door opened and she felt people pulling her out, somebody taking Sarah away again. Her feet tripped and stumbled as she got carried to a place that smelled of antiseptic. Then she was shoved down on a bed. Somebody was talking to her, asking her questions. She struggled to make sense of them, struggled to make sense of where she was. A light was flashed into her eyes, blinding her. She put her arms up to fight against it.

Where was Sarah? She needed to get Sarah. She screamed for her baby, screamed for her child. She lashed out with her hand and struck somebody on the face. She watched him roll backwards, but somebody else came in. She felt her arms being restrained. There came an injection, an injection that went in somewhere. She could feel a needle, but she struggled to ascertain just where.

Then there came sleep, a darkness wafting over her. Peace and quiet. That was all she knew, nothing more, nothing less, until her eyes flicked open again. Everything was white above. She rolled her head. It was white to her left. She rolled again. It was white to her right. She looked down and the clothes she'd been wearing when she got home weren't there. She was in some sort of basic gown. Someone was standing up on the far side of the room and saying something to her. 'Alice,' were the words. 'Alice.' She was Alice. Did they not know she was Alice?

'Tell me,' said Alice, 'tell me.' Then she had to stop. There was nothing there. She tried again, 'Alice. Alice.' Alice's head swam, but she managed to roll it up and look over at the woman who was talking to her.

'Where is Sarah? Where is Sarah?' asked Alice. 'I need Sarah.' She watched the woman step forward, her face coming more into view. She bent down and leaned over Alice.

'I'm sorry,' said the woman. Alice could see the tears in her eyes. She didn't have to say anymore.

Chapter 17

Macleod, sitting behind his desk, growled at the DCI as he marched into his office. Seoras knew it was coming because the man was keen on Lamb as a suspect. Now that another mother had walked in with a dead child, he was desperate to have him brought in.

'You go out and you bring Lamb in now for questioning.'

'Okay,' said Macleod, which took the DCI somewhat aback, giving the man's face a shocked look. The shoulders that had been lifted up in anger and determination suddenly slumped. 'Okay, but he didn't do it. But if you want me to, I'll bring him in. I'll go through the motions.'

'What makes you so sure?' asked Lawson. 'What makes you so sure that Lamb wasn't out there doing this?'

'Because he's an obsessive, but the woman he's obsessed with was upstairs, not out there. When you look at how he organises things, it's a mess. Even upstairs, the flat that's left empty, you can go up and use it. But what? Soak the front of it? What good is that going to do, put people off from going in? People wouldn't be going in anyway unless there's some business, and then beyond that, everything's just left all over the floor. He doesn't even know how to cover up his own tracks. He's left behind, so to speak, DNA evidence on the paper. He has holes that he hasn't really covered up, in any shape, sense, or form. The least you would do is stick them all behind some pictures or something. He's not got it in him to be able to plan something like this. We're going to the crime scenes and we're not finding DNA. We're talking about somebody that knows what they're doing. Although in truth, I think we're talking about a lot of people that know what they're doing.'

'A lot of people?'

'Yes, each one different,' said Macleod.

'But the motive's the same. There's the mother with the child, killed the child, put the symbols on the child,' said Lawson, 'and then leave the mother back in some disorientated state. The first one just went wrong.'

'Yes, the first one just went wrong. So, Lamb, who's already had relations with Amanda then decides that he's going to simply expand his lusts. No, this is somebody else who's slipped up following a template. The second one loses himself in the moment with the mother. The third one does it exactly right,' said Macleod.

'Nonsense,' said Lawson. 'Three different people would soon screw it up.'

'One did. Left some DNA at the scene, didn't he? I'm sure Jona will get hold of that soon enough.'

'Regardless, get Lamb in, and don't hold back in the questions. As far as I'm concerned, he's our main suspect. In fact, I want to sit in on it.'

'Let's go get him then,' said Macleod. He stood up, calmly walked around the desk, put his coat on. 'Let's go get him.'

'Are you taking the mick out of me, Inspector?'

'No, sir,' Macleod said slowly and deliberately. 'But you're asking me to go against every good piece of judgment I've got in me. Frankly, it's a waste of our time.'

Apoplectic was not a word that Macleod was accustomed to use, but having seen the reaction of his DCI, he thought it probably was justified in this instance.

'I've had enough of this, Macleod. Get down to that car.' Lawson opened the door of Macleod's office and shouted over to Hope. 'McGrath, with me now.'

Hope spun around, looked at him, watching as the DCI marched out of the room. Macleod came through his office door in his coat and Hope gave him a look.

'I thought he was all about first-name terms.'

'I don't think I'm on the Christmas card list then,' said Macleod. 'He wants us to pick up Lamb. You'd better come. You wouldn't want your boss getting lifted for having carried out a murder himself.' Hope narrowed her eyes at Macleod, said something to Ross, and turned back for her coat.

'Where's Clarissa anyway?' asked Macleod.

'Out and about, sir. She's tailing a potential suspect.'

'Tailing?' said Macleod.

'Yes, sir. It's a Dr Forbes. He seems to have a lot of information on the occult. Came out of our visit to those guys who work for Ross on the industrial estate.'

'The internet geeks? Those ones?' said Macleod.

'Yes, sir. Forbes is a potential person of interest. He's possibly a suspect. I'm not entirely sure. Clarissa went to start kicking down some doors.'

'Very good,' said Macleod. 'Come on, Hope. Let's go before the DCI explodes.'

Half an hour later, Macleod stood rapping the door of Ian Lamb's flat. The man opened it, dressed in a cardigan with slippers. He still had half a piece of toast in his mouth, chewing on it in a rather angry fashion when he saw them there.

'What's this?' he said. 'This doesn't look good, not with people around here asking about us neighbours. Amanda's neighbours this, Amanda's neighbours that. Any of us dodgy.'

'Can we speak inside, sir?' asked Macleod.

'Do we have to?'

'Probably better than on the doorstep. The press will still be about here and there.'

'What is the hold-up? Just get it done here.'

The DCI pushed past Macleod, pulled out his warrant card, and held it up in front of Lamb's face. 'Ian Lamb, I'm taking you in for questioning regarding the recent murders. Kindly come down to the station with me.'

'Why?' asked Lamb. 'I haven't done anything. Well, I know what I did upstairs wasn't right, but other than that, I haven't done anything.'

'Where were you yesterday?' asked Macleod.

'I was here all the time on my own. I had to keep the curtains closed as well. The press are annoying buggers, come up and put the camera right in the window. Somebody got a shot of me eating my toast and beans.'

'You're coming with us,' said the DCI. 'Kindly get your coat.'

'You think I'm a suspect?' blurted Lamb. Macleod could hear over his shoulder a bit of commotion. Somebody shouted, 'Come on. They're taking somebody in.' Macleod turned to look over his shoulder and several cameras were pointed at him. As the circus continued to grow, Macleod watched as the DCI took Lamb in for questioning in front of all the media cameras. It felt like they had been called there. When he first arrived, he was struggling to catch a glimpse of them. Suddenly, every channel going was there.

* * *

Clarissa Urquhart parked the small green car and watched Dr Forbes step out of his BMW and walk towards what was described as a boarding house by the sign outside the building. As he came towards the front steps, the door was opened for him and he made his way inside while Clarissa watched from the street. Once he'd gone through, she took a photograph of the sign, realising it was for a men-only boarding house where rooms were available at a reasonable price.

This seemed somewhat antiquated and she wondered if it was just simply a cover, so she marched over, shawl wrapped around her against the cold she was feeling. Clarissa pressed the doorbell after climbing up a large number of steps to the front door. The door was opened and a rather tall man wearing a doorman's outfit looked her up and down, almost out of curiosity.

'Hi, I'd like to inquire about some rooms,' said Carissa.

'I'm afraid, madam, that the rooms here are only for rent to a male clientele.'

'Are you sure you can do that?' asked Clarissa. 'I thought with equality now, we had to hire them out to everyone.'

'I assure you that the rooms here are for male clientele only. Is there anything else I can help you with, madam?'

Clarissa watched him stare down at her. He was well over six-foot, broad shoulders too, and she wondered why he got the doorman's job because he looked more like a bouncer.

She thought about pulling a warrant card out, thought about demanding access, marching up to see what Dr Forbes was up to but she decided instead not to, because that would break cover. He'd know she was onto him, know she was after whatever it was he was doing.

'Well, I'm sorry to disturb you,' said Clarissa, and the man looked at her as if he hadn't been disturbed at all.

'I believe there's a woman's guest house two streets down around the corner.'

Clarissa thought about the place he was talking about and realised it was a women's refuge. She was inclined to tell him it wasn't the same thing but thought it better if she looked like she wasn't from the area. So, she simply thanked him before walking back to the green car.

As she sat looking up at the building, she saw Dr Forbes suddenly at a window looking down at the street. He hadn't clocked her car. He hadn't clocked anything about her. He was simply scanning here, there, and everywhere. Soon, another man arrived at the front door and was let in. He was short and stocky. Then a tall gentleman, then a rotund one. They were all at that front door within five minutes of each other, and they were followed by four more.

While it was perfectly conceivable that there were enough flats in there for each of them to have their own, the arrival of them all at the same time told Clarissa that this was a meeting of some sort. Her problem was that it was up on the top floor, some three floors up.

She looked at the side of the house, such an old building that it had bits and pieces lumbering off it, almost like the growth that had sprouted out over the edges. Then an idea formed in Clarissa's head. If she went round to the back, got up onto the wall, she could get onto the lowest roof, and from that roof, she could relocate up to another roof and then another one and she could probably look in the window that was at the side where Dr Forbes had looked out. She'd be able to see what was going on. Maybe even she'd be able to hear.

Clarissa wished that Hope was here. She was more suited to climbing up. Seoras couldn't do it. Ross would give it a go, but in truth, this was something made for Hope. However, she wasn't here so there was no one but the woman sat in the sports car to deal with this.

Clarissa walked quietly round to the rear of the house and looked at the wall before her. It was tall so she hauled a nearby bin over and clambered up on top of it, then climbed onto the wall. In her day, she could balance well, and in fact, she'd even been a ballet dancer at one point; but she felt that that counted for little as she tried to step across onto the next roof.

It was corrugated, looked like it covered a shed, and she walked where she saw the roof had been screwed down, trying to follow the roof beams. From there, she was up and onto another roof, again stretching and pulling herself onto it. She finally reached the last section where it took her two tries to swing her leg up, catch it with the inside of her boot, and then haul herself up.

By the time she got near the window, she was out of breath and she had to compose herself before peering in. Inside, she saw Dr Forbes addressing the gathering before they all stood up and began to chant in a low hum. It continued for at least two minutes, but each man seemed to know how it went. The group then sat down, and Clarissa could just about hear Dr Forbes telling everyone that someone would no longer be attending. Someone had not adhered to the practices of the group. Someone had screwed up, literally.

Clarissa became aware as she peered in that the group were

looking at someone who had clearly done something wrong. There was no symbology on any of them that she could see, albeit that was only three people. Most of the group were obscured but she thought if she moved position, she may be able to see more but the roof under her feet was slanted and it was slippery. She was also wary of making a noise because up here, she would be struggling to get away cleanly, and she'd have to explain why someone like her was listening in to a conversation three floors up.

The men began to chant and she saw Forbes looking at the condemned man, beyond Clarissa's view, Forbes's face angry. He began to speak in a language she didn't understand, wondering if it was Latin. Many of the men stood arms crossed, folded against the man, and slowly they began to turn their back. She'd have to be quick before they turned to the window.

Desperately, she lifted a foot, put it higher up the roof, and tried to drag herself up, but her foot slipped. She came down hard on her shoulder and began to slide down off the roof. She hit the second roof that she climbed up on previously and it began to slant away. She tumbled, spinning several times before coming off it, smacking into another roof with a hard thwack.

Clarissa threw her arms out desperately, unsure just where she was and what was happening. Her feet slipped off the end of another roof, but her hands grabbed onto something. It was guttering and it was bending. She couldn't fall off. She'd break something, come down hard, and be left there. She could hear a commotion from upstairs. She'd already made a racket.

Clarissa's feet scrabbled, kicking forward, and she began to swing on the guttering. She couldn't see below her, so desperate was she to hang on with what was above. She was disoriented having spun and fallen several times. Her shoulder ached, and she felt the fingers going, slipping out of the guttering as it bent backward.

No, no, no, no, she thought, *Don't, don't, don't, don't, don't let go, no.*

Both hands let it go at the same time, the gutter, like some slippery fish, she couldn't keep a hold of, and she dropped. Landing about two feet further down, her ankle jarred. The distance she had dropped was nothing.

She turned to get out of the way, and she heard the front door of the house being opened. Her ankle was smarting, and she began to limp off. Clarissa quickly cut back in behind the shed she had initially jumped up onto and ran in behind the house by the outer wall.

At the end, she could see a gate, found it to be a simple latch, opened it, and stepped out onto the street, but realised they wouldn't be daft. Surely, they'd follow her out to here. Clarissa hobbled across the narrow road, and she heard the gate opening behind her. She couldn't go left or right on the street, they'd see her. Instead, having reached the other side, she pitched herself over a small wall that was at knee height and landed just beyond a bed of pansies.

The grass around her was damp, but she got onto her knees and with her elbows marched along until she was behind a large hedge. She tried to immerse herself into it, but she wasn't sure how good a job she did and then froze as she heard voices on the street.

'Must have run off. Who was it anyway?'

'Don't know,' said somebody.

'There was a woman at the door, sir.' It was the voice of the doorman. 'But to be honest, she couldn't have got up there.'

Clarissa smiled, happy to have defied the odds again. She'd paid for it and she could feel the ankle swelling up. It was sore despite the small drop she'd descended, and her shoulders and legs had taken a pounding during the fall.

She waited until they disappeared, then stood up rather painfully, brushing down her shawl. Clarissa hobbled down the driveway of the house, wondered if anyone was in, but instead kept walking until she reached the rear garden and saw a fence at the back with a gate in it. Walking through it, she found another side street and identified exactly where she was. It took her another ten minutes to get back to the car.

What to make of it? she thought, *what to make of it. Something was afoot. Forbes was something, a leader of sorts.* She put her foot down on the accelerator and instantly yelped; her ankle wasn't going to mend easy.

Chapter 18

Macleod stood up from the chair, took another look at Ian Lamb, and then walked from the interview room. As he pushed open the door, out into the corridor beyond, he was immediately accosted by DCI Lawson.

'Surely there's more. What are you coming out for, man?'

Macleod looked down at the man, being a slight bit smaller, and shook his head. 'You can go round and round in circles, Chief Inspector, but that man's not guilty. That man's a lot of things, but he's not a killer.'

'You're not asking him the right questions. You need to be tough, get him running.'

'No,' said Macleod. 'I need to ascertain where he was and what he was doing. I believe I've done that.'

'No, you haven't. You haven't pressurised him enough. That man knows something. We need to be on it.'

'If that's the way you feel about it, I'm off for a coffee and a sit down, and then I'll go back in after that, but frankly I don't know where else to go with it.'

'Maybe McGrath should take over the questioning.'

Macleod didn't even look round at Hope for he knew what

response she would give.

'Chief Inspector, with all due respect, this is Detective Inspector Macleod's case. For what it's worth, I agree with Seoras. This man didn't do it. We can ask more questions if you wish.'

'He was there at the start of this. He can't account for where he was for the other murders. He was looking in at Amanda Hughes. Who's to say he wasn't looking in on any of the others?'

'The fact he hasn't been found to be looking in on anyone else.'

'Macleod, we've got three dead. You've got an obvious suspect there. You need to get the truth out of him.'

'I already have.'

Macleod stormed off, and as Hope went to follow him, Lawson barred her path with his arm. 'Don't go down with him,' he said. 'Don't let your loyalty get in the way. There's a guilty man in there, and if you work this right, you'll come out smelling of roses.'

Hope shook her head. 'I need a coffee, too.' McGrath stood up to her full height and looked down at the DCI. 'I've already told you my opinion.'

Hope found Macleod in the canteen and wondered why he wasn't in his office. Regardless, she walked up to the hatch, asked for a coffee, and then sat down beside her boss.

'Before you ask, he won't come here. He won't have a scene in here. He'd have it down in the interview rooms, he'd have it in my office, he'd have it in his office, but he doesn't wash dirty laundry in public that much. If he has it out down here, he'll be worried I'll have a go at him.'

'Easy,' said Hope. 'You're getting riled with him.'

149

'Of course, I'm getting riled with him,' said Macleod. 'He's all over me. All over me. Ian Lamb this, Ian Lamb that. Ian hasn't got a clue about these murders.'

'There's certainly no evidence to back it up.'

Macleod flicked his head. 'No, there's more than that. There's more than that, Hope. Don't go like this.'

'Go like what?' she said. 'I've backed you up out there. Do you know what he told me? He told me I could make a name for myself and not to be clinging on to your shirt tails, not to back you in this way. I've backed you, Seoras. I'll always back you. If I don't agree with you, I tell you straight, but I think you're right on this one.'

She watched Macleod hang his head. 'Yes,' he said. 'Yes.'

'What's up?' asked Hope.

'Three of them. Three of them and we aren't anywhere. We're nowhere, Hope. I don't care that he's got me running around after Ian Lamb, other than it's a complete waste of my time. Outside of that, I do not care. He's the boss, and if he wants this and he wants that, then he'll get it. The only reason I'm getting down at the moment is I don't have anywhere else to go. Ross is looking into the background. We've got nothing to hang the women together other than they have kids. They have kids of a certain age, young enough that they're easily handled, and all of the mothers have been taken out in some way, put under, removed. We have someone who's cut symbols, but not symbols of a particular cult, just several symbols from different mythologies. All done with a knife, and yet, Jona's telling me they're done with different pressures.'

'Has she come back with the report on the third victim.'

'Similar type of knife we reckon, but not done by the same hand, she thinks. Of course, the boss won't believe that, and she can't be completely conclusive on it either. It's just what she's seeing, just what she thinks. Then if you tell him that, he screams copycat. There's no copycat here. We didn't let the symbols get out. The newspapers didn't carry it. The news didn't carry it. It's just, it's just . . .'

'Seoras, stop. Stop. You're losing it. I'm telling you, you're losing it.'

'Blooming right, I'm losing it. It looks like I was wrong.'

Hope looked up to see Macleod was staring ahead at the DCI entering the canteen area.

'Macleod, get back down in there.' Clearly the man had gone hunting for Macleod, and then only wound up in the canteen after checking the other areas Macleod had distinctly avoided.

'There's nothing to hold him with. He's clean as a whistle regarding the murders. There's nothing. The only thing I've got is circumstantial, and when I say circumstantial, it's barely that. We've got him as a peeping Tom, as a leery individual. He's got no connection to the other two victims.'

'I'm giving you a direct order. You keep that man in the cells. He doesn't come out. You understand?'

'You keep him in the cells. You put the order through.'

'I don't know who you think you are. I don't care if you're on the front of newspapers, if people here think you've solved cases before. I'm the DCI. I'm your boss, and I'm telling you, you keep him in. Now, get back down there and get interviewing that man.'

'No,' said Macleod, 'because frankly, it's a complete waste of our time.'

'You'll get down there, and I'm coming down to watch.'

'No,' said Macleod. 'We need to be looking at all our avenues. We need to find out where the killer's coming from. Why is there a group of them? What is happening?'

'Sergeant McGrath, accompany me down; we begin questioning Ian Lamb again.'

Macleod stared up at the DCI, 'You've just got to jump in, you've just got to barge in because I disagree with you.'

'I'm telling you to get down and get on him.'

'If you set him up as a suspect, if you put him up as a main contender here . . .' started Macleod.

'He is our only contender at the moment, and for that, we will get in, and we will make sure that we find out how he did it.'

'I'm sure, sir,' said Hope, 'that the idea is that we find out whether he did it, not how he did it.'

'Just keep your nose out of this, Sergeant. You're good for this department. Strong female making her way up the ranks; don't blow it by firing guns across me.' Hope went to speak, but Macleod put his hand up.

'Thank you, Hope. You're, of course correct, but the DCI will not see that. He is correct. Don't put yourself in jeopardy for this. It's my investigation, and I carry the can for it, and I will tell the DCI that Ian Lamb did not do it. I'll go and pull my team together, and we'll go through the evidence again. So far, no one on my team is seeing him as our killer. When we bring ourselves together and discuss it, I'll look for a new avenue to attack. If you want me to keep him in the cells until then, that's fine, I'll do it,' said Macleod. 'I'll do it, as much as it's wrong and against that man's freedom and liberty, I'll do it. Now, kindly let me drink my coffee in peace.'

The DCI felt that one but marched out of the canteen, turning several times to look at Macleod. The canteen was reasonably full, and a number of other people could be heard whispering once DCI Lawson walked away. Hope stood up and looked around.

'Really? Really? No, we're not discussing this. We're not going to chat about it like this. We're professionals, this is a professional disagreement, get back to work.'

'That was a bit strong,' said Macleod under his breath.

'People needed to be put in their place; you don't sit and talk about bosses like that.'

'Bosses don't come down here and have a discussion like that,' said Macleod. 'Whatever shortcomings, I understand Ian Lamb is the only tangible link in here at the moment, and Lawson still wants him to be the killer. So do I, Hope, but he's not; he really isn't. Whatever circus is going on outside, we'll have to keep them out of our thoughts. We'll pull the team together, sit down, and have a proper chat about it.'

The door of the canteen burst open. Clarissa Urquhart dragged herself across the floor, her right leg obviously causing pain, as she limped towards Macleod.

'Are you all right?' he asked.

'Do I look sodding all right? Do I walk like this? No. We've all been sitting around having coffee.'

Macleod let it go. He could tell from the way Clarissa was walking that she was really struggling.

'Have you had that checked out?'

'No, I haven't had it checked out. I've come here to see you, and believe it or not, I'm not looking for your medical opinion.'

'Probably a little bit quieter would be best,' said Hope.

'What?' blurted Clarissa.

'We've just had a blowout here between the DCI and the inspector; ears are listening. Probably best we don't have one right now.'

'You're telling me I have to walk all the way up those stairs, up to the office before I can tell you stuff?'

'Hope's right,' said Macleod, 'but she's going to give you a hand up there.'

By the time the three of them had relocated to Macleod's office, Clarissa was in real pain. Hope disappeared off to get her a couple of paracetamol, and the woman sat breathing heavily while Macleod stared at her.

'What?' she asked.

'You're not the actual hound of the unit; you know that.'

'How dare you,' she said; 'I can hold my own.'

'All I'm saying is you can take a little bit of backup with you. Somebody like Hope, Ross even.'

'I didn't think I'd be climbing up over roofs.'

'What are you climbing over roofs for?'

'Wait,' she said, 'wait until Hope gets back.'

Two minutes later, Clarissa took Macleod and Hope through what had happened, pointing out in extreme detail where she'd hung on and then fallen a reasonable distance to the ground, landing on her ankle and hurting it. She didn't want them to know it was only two feet, but she talked about hiding in the bushes and crawling along the garden of the house behind the one she'd been investigating. Macleod juked around his desk to see her muddy knees.

'What did you figure out?'

'Dr Forbes, he's somehow involved in it. There were a group of men turning their back on someone.'

'Turning their back?' queried Macleod.

'He spoke in a different language. I don't know what type of language it was. Possibly . . .'

'Possibly what?'

154

'Latin. I'm not an expert. I mean when you were looking at the art world, and you get Latin inscribed on something, I have to go look it up properly. It's not what I do, but I swear it was Latin.'

'A group of men met at the top of a house, they had a meeting, they spoke Latin, and they weren't happy with somebody who's not coming back to the meeting, and you fell off the roof. Is that what you're telling me?' said Macleod.

'He's into this symbology; he's into this group. This could be Dark Union; this could be the Dark Union group.'

'It could be,' said Hope, 'except we've got absolutely no evidence. You know that Dr Forbes is possibly into symbology and cults; you know he met with a group of people in an upstairs room. You know that their society, whatever it is, has got a problem with a member. There's nothing illegal in there. There's nothing we could pin and say they did it. I know you risked a lot, Clarissa, but we haven't got much there,' said Hope.

'Certainly haven't got anything I can take to the DCI and get him off my back,' said Macleod. 'It's a channel to go down, one to keep pursuing, but the first thing you're going to do is go and get that ankle looked at; understood?'

'Understood,' said Clarissa.

'Only after you come and sit in a meeting with the rest of us,' said Macleod.

'I thought you cared for a moment.'

Chapter 19

Macleod was sombre as he sat at the small round table with the rest of the team in front of him. Everything sat heavy on him. He didn't like not having a decent relationship with the DCI. The man had only been in recently, but Macleod saw him caving very quickly to the pressure around him. Of course, everyone wanted this cleaned up quickly. Of course, they wanted whoever was doing it to stop, but putting pressure on an innocent man, who McGrath also considered to be the wrong person, didn't help.

Sure, you could tell people up above you, 'We were processing; we were chasing down a lead,' but with few other leads, that wasn't easy. But there were other leads, albeit, less obvious. Clarissa had Dr Forbes and his group. There was also a knife. A knife they could look at, a knife they could find the origin of. There were other things to do, and he needed to get his team doing them.

He needed to present these things to the DCI, get the ideas out in the open so Lawson could see what was going on in his mind. Macleod was a very self-contained person. He knew that and sometimes he needed to open up more about what he was thinking. His biggest problem was he didn't trust the DCI and he got the feeling Hope didn't either.

'So, Ian Lamb,' said Macleod. 'What have we got in his internet records?'

Ross gave a brief cough. 'As I said last time, yes, he likes his pornography. Yes, he's a man who clearly had something for Amanda Hughes, but I've got nothing occultic on him, nothing on the dark web. He doesn't go anywhere. I've got nothing. Bank accounts, gone through them. There's just no link into anything of a methodical or occultic nature. I'm at a dead end. The geeks, as you politely called them, are at a dead end. We're at a dead end with everything about him.'

'He doesn't look like a person who can handle a knife,' said Hope. 'The upstairs flat that he was living out of watching her, that place was a mess. He doesn't look to be somebody who can conduct himself well.'

'The killer would have to be organised,' said Jona. 'Forensically, we're not picking up anything. We're not getting any DNA from these killers and yet Ian Lamb left DNA around here, there, and everywhere. You have to be taught these patterns too. You have to be very good at it.'

'Taught,' said Macleod, 'like be in that sort of field.'

'Not necessarily,' said Jona, 'but you would've had to have the training that we have. We know what to look for. Therefore, people not leaving forensic evidence around, would know that as well. I'm not saying they must be in the service, in the force, or anything like that, but they would have to have some sort of training, some sort of idea. I get the feeling that Ian Lamb hasn't had any of that.'

'Going through his history, I don't see any of that,' said Ross. 'He's a dead duck when it comes to being a potential killer.'

'So, we're all of the same opinion here. Ian Lamb is not our killer.'

'I think I speak for all of us, Seoras,' said Clarissa. 'Can we stop talking about Ian Lamb and let's start talking about what we can do?'

'The DCI is all over us on Ian Lamb. I'm sorry, but I have to be dotting the Is and crossing the Ts. I'm afraid that may not be enough. I think the DCI's looking for something to keep everybody off his back.'

'I thought that was his job,' said Clarissa, 'to keep everybody off our back.'

'Doesn't look like it,' said Hope. 'As far as I can tell, he can't.'

'Stop,' said Macleod. 'We don't do this. He's my problem. Okay? He's my problem. Whatever support we need, whatever he needs to be doing for us, that's my problem and you, in return, don't talk about him. Not like that. I grew up in a police force with respect. A lot of other problems, but with respect. You show respect.'

'Sorry, sir,' said Ross. The man hadn't even said anything, and he was apologising for the group.

'I wasn't exactly looking at you, Ross.' Macleod glanced over at Clarissa and then at Hope.

'Understood,' said Hope.

'Well, if he was doing his . . .'

'Enough, Clarissa,' said Macleod, 'but while we're on it, what about this knife?'

'Well, let me talk through it with Jona,' said Clarissa. 'It appears that it is quite ornate, and I reckon it's come from underground dealers. Takes quite a steady hand to carve with it. It's not something everybody would use and certainly, not everybody could use it that well. Well, I say that well . . .'

'As I said to Clarissa,' said Jona, 'and to yourself, the cuts were not as good on the second body. I also think the first and the third aren't the same. It's hard to quantify this, hard to put it down in black and white. It's not a hunch. It's just an observation but it's not one that I can be definitive about, especially regarding the first and the third carving. Could they be done by the same person? Yes, as could the second one. Maybe they were just rushed. Maybe they were just under more stress for whatever reason.'

'But,' said Macleod, 'you personally believe it was three different people?'

'Very much,' said Jona. 'I can put that in their report, but ultimately, there's no evidence to show it. It's just a belief.'

'That's understood,' said Macleod. 'But we really need to be sure of that and it will get Ian Lamb out of the way on the other murders.' He looked back to Clarissa. 'As you were saying.'

'Well, Seoras,' said Clarissa, 'the thing is with it,' and she stood up, pressed a button showing the knife up on a screen, 'if you look at the handle marks, there's occultic symbols on it but this is rare, this knife. I haven't seen one quite like this, ever.'

'Did you ever work in that field,' asked Macleod.

'Came across it several times, but there are plenty of knives in the world that can do a lot of damage up close, ones that are meant to be used on a symbolic victim. Certainly, in the past, when cultures would carve out hearts and all that sort of thing.'

Macleod watched the disdain on her face but then Clarissa rallied. 'It would be underground dealers. Underground dealers and you'd probably pay a packet for it. Sales would be cash so it's difficult to trace but things like this, you don't move them about without causing some sort of noise. Some people would know about it. I can chase this line, I can go with this like you said but to be frank, it's going to take time. It's not like I'm going to come back tomorrow with it. I'm going to have to go places. I'm going to have to see people. I'm going to be less available here, Seoras, and with the way temperatures are rising.'

'What do you mean temperatures are rising?' asked Macleod. 'You've been in this situation before?'

'Have you watched the news? Have you caught any of this?'

'I haven't really had an awful lot of time to check the news.'

Clarissa stood up, went over and grabbed the remote control from the TV. She put on the main news channel. Macleod suddenly realised that National News were now reporting on these murders across the UK, not just in Scotland. He watched and saw the DCI taking in Ian Lamb, he and Hope accompanying him from behind and then there proceeded to be a roundtable discussion about whether Ian Lamb was the killer and then a rather half-hazard effort at actually addressing who he was.

Then something happened that caused Macleod to drop his jaw. They reported that he had been in the upstairs room watching Amanda Hughes through small holes and the wall. They reported that the room was full of pornography and the man was quite a leery individual.

'How did that get out?' asked Macleod. He glanced over at Jona.

'Not from my lot. Never,' she said.

'Is it still sealed off?' asked Hope. 'Wouldn't be that difficult to leak? You could whip somebody up there as we're not going to have people there anymore, are we?'

160

'We might have people looking out for Ian Lamb,' suggested Clarissa.

'I want to know where that came from,' said Macleod. 'I want to know who's pushing the public towards Ian Lamb. That never should have come out. He's not in the frame, is he? It's all circumstantial and even those things are not that circumstantial. There are things you hold up as a red rag to a bull to go, "Look, here we go. Pervert. Must have killed kids and mom." I'm not having it. I'm absolutely not having it.'

He stood up and thumped the desk, turned around and walked to the back of the room. Then he spun around, suddenly looking at them all again. 'We need to get onto this quick. We need to get tight with who did it; otherwise, Ian Lamb is going to be in trouble.'

'Probably deserves it,' said Clarissa but Macleod railed back.

'No, he doesn't. He doesn't deserve it. He's made whatever choices, created whatever sort of space, but he does not deserve to be tarnished with a label of killer and especially not a child killer. You know as well as I, if he goes in anywhere, that man will not be able to stand it. That man will be finished off in a prison. I've just sat down with Hope interviewing him. That man is a mess. He's only just beginning to realise the scrutiny he's going to come under, and he wet himself. And we took him out through the press scrum.'

'The boss is right on that one, too,' said Hope. 'There's no way that man will survive inside. Now they're bringing out all the sexual stuff and started asking if he interfered with the kids.'

'Well, he didn't,' said Jona. 'There's none of that. There's only the one incidence and that's with the mother.'

'We've got a sample from him, haven't we?'

'No,' said Jona,' we haven't. I've only got the one DNA trace and that's Sandra Mackay.'

'But I thought that he'd had relations with her. I thought that you could . . .'

'How do we put this? There was no evidence left behind. I checked her body and stuff but the only DNA that's coming off her is her own.'

'How's that possible,' asked Macleod. 'You go to bed with somebody, you'll leave your DNA all over them, surely.'

'If not in them,' said Clarissa.'

Macleod glanced over at the crude comment.

'They may have had sex but he certainly didn't leave anything behind. I didn't find anything on the body. It's very confusing,' said Jona, 'very confusing but I can't find anything. No other DNA there. Nothing to say that somebody else was involved with her. Clearly, there was, since she seems to think that there was.'

'Because if there was, that would have nailed Ian Lamb if he'd done it. If he hadn't, he'd been in the clear.'

'Do you think this has got something to do with what I saw?' asked Clarissa. 'That's also what I don't understand. How do we go from the person being kicked out for a mistake to the three kids being murdered. We have a mistake being made in that somebody slept with mum, or at least we think they did.'

'True,' said Macleod, 'but the mistake would've revealed them. So then how on earth is there no DNA?'

'It sounds plausible,' said Hope, 'but there's no evidence. It's circumstantial. At the moment, we need to get onto these other lines of enquiry. Maybe you should take it to the DCI. Maybe you should tell them about these.'

'It's not like I haven't tried,' said Macleod. 'Besides, just what

I said, we're not here to discuss the DCI. We're here to discuss what we're doing.'

'Well, in that case, what do you want me to do to?' asked Clarissa.

'If your foot's not too bad, I want you to go and hunt down this lead. I can't afford to send Ross and Hope away with you. Hope's going to be tied up with me trying to stop Ian Lamb from getting the blame of all of this. It's also quite a loose chase you're going on. Keep in contact with Ross. He can help you with finding a lot of this stuff on the net.'

'Okay,' said Clarissa. 'I'll do it but understand this is not going to be quick. I'll also try and dig up from my head the faces I saw at that meeting. See if I can ID any of them.'

'You can try, but it might be quite hard. I'm not sure anyone's going to be a criminal,' said Ross.

'That's true,' said Macleod. 'In the meantime, let's go back over the three child murders. Let's dig out for more witnesses. Troll through again. Let's put out some more officers stopping cars, finding out what they know. We need something to drop,' said Macleod. 'That's what we need now. We haven't got anything. We need to be patient.'

'I don't think too many people are going to be patient, Seoras,' said Hope, her head nodding at the TV screen. The sound was off but more and more pictures of the crime scenes from a distance were being run.

'We'll need to keep a tight lead on this,' said Macleod. 'If they find out about the symbology, this could explode. Bad enough they already think there's a sex-crazed man committing this.'

Chapter 20

Hope walked out of Macleod's office shaking her head. It was hard enough working a job like this without people pulling strings from the outside. The main focus should always be to find out who killed whoever, try to bring the killer to justice, but that was never the case, was it? There were always other parties involved, always other parties looking to drive their own agendas.

The press wanted their story, and a character like Ian Lamb with his appetites and lust painted a great picture for them, one with which to scare the public. There was no evidence that Ian had ever sought to harm any young children, but for some reason he was being targeted. The difficulty always was you had to be sure you didn't get it wrong, had to be convinced that the evidence didn't sit against the man. In truth, it didn't. The knife had been found at a leisure centre which he frequented, but that made no sense to Hope at all. Why would he dump the knife there? A place he'd been, a place where he walked in on CCTV through the front door. The last thing you would do if you dumped the knife was to be seen anywhere near it.

She descended the stairs down towards the canteen, aware she hadn't actually eaten that day. Walking in, she could hear the odd murmur and mutter, probably coming back from the incident earlier on. She shook it off, walked over to the self-service and started to pick out a salad before deciding that it was actually the worst decision going. She wanted something hot and filling. *Steak pie,* she thought. *Steak pie and potatoes with gravy and throw a load of veg on top of it.*

It took another minute before she sat down with her ironic diet cola and began to tuck into the steak pie in front of her. There were words still being said. She saw people looking over at her, but she ignored them. It wasn't becoming for any officer to talk like that. If they had something to say, they could come and see her; otherwise, they could forget it.

The thing about Hope was she'd had plenty of training in this sense. When she came up through the ranks, people had always said it was because of her good looks and size. Not many women were six feet with red hair, and while she was quite happy to take the compliment about her looks, she was never happy for it to be used to say why she got where she was. Seoras had never done that. Once Seoras and she had seen eye to eye, she'd always felt valued by him, always felt she was where she was because of what he saw in her. Sure, they had times along the route, times when he thought she wasn't ready, but he still saw her as the one to take over from him. Not that that was always a choice he would get.

The team seemed to be struggling on. Ross was quite obviously upset, but they were dealing with child murder, and he remained professional as ever. It must strike him though, she thought, as he's looking to become a father. You've got somebody taking away that right, taking away those who could be parented. She wasn't sure how she'd deal with it. Kids had never come up between her and John, although in truth, they were still in such early days.

Macleod was moody, very moody. It wasn't the children's deaths that were bothering him, although, of course, it was taking a toll, as was everything else around it. The main gripe was they couldn't get any traction, and that was the thing about Seoras. He didn't get angry with people. He'd get angry at the situation, frustrated at the lack of movement, but if it wasn't there, it wasn't there.

Clarissa, on the other hand, was clearly being affected. Since when did she jump up onto roofs, so eager not to miss anything, so eager not to give away the chance of finding out about someone? She jumped up on a roof and nearly wrecked her leg. She said she'd rolled down, bounced, hung on. These weren't things she should be doing. These were the things Hope should be doing.

Hope looked up as the canteen door opened and saw the DCI walking towards her. Alan Lawson always looked impressive in a suit. For somebody so small, he obviously had good tailoring for it never looked like it was all over him. Instead, it was always neat and dapper. With his golden locks, she was sure some women would've been deeply attracted by him. Not Hope though; the man was so much smaller than she was. She'd seen bigger golf clubs to use. She put her head back down and began eating some more of her pie before she heard the scrape of the chair and Alan Lawson sat down beside her.

'Do you mind if I join you?'

'Looks like you already have,' said Hope, 'but if you want.'

She had to be careful. She wasn't like Macleod. If they kicked him out, well, his retirement pension would be there. He could live quite happily off it. He'd be bored, wouldn't know what to do with himself, but outside of that, he'd be financially comfortable. Hope, on the other hand, would have to go find another job. She was actually quite happy with this one, so she didn't intend to cheese off her DCI too much.

'Oh, sorry to bother you, but I really could do with your understanding,' said Lawson. 'I just want to understand about Macleod's thinking.'

Hope looked around her and saw the staring faces looking over.

'I'm not sure this is wise, sir.'

'It's Alan Lawson. Just Alan will do. We've given up all that stuff. I noticed Macleod still makes Ross call him sir.'

'Macleod doesn't make Ross call him anything. Ross decides to call the inspector sir. He'll call you sir as well.'

'He did. He wouldn't change either.'

'No, it's just a thing with Ross.'

'You all call him Ross as well.'

'Yes, because he likes it.'

'Is he all right?'

'What do you mean, "Is he all right?"' asked Hope. 'Alan Ross is one of the best officers we've got. He's a wizard. The department wouldn't run well without him because he picks up all the loose stuff. Makes sure all the I's are dotted and the T's are crossed. He also happens to rock a computer, and he's a very good friend. Once again, what do you mean by "Is he all right?"'

'Nothing. Nothing. Sorry, I shouldn't be thinking like that, but I do want to know about Macleod's thinking.'

'Probably not here though,' said Hope.

'Why?' asked the DCI.

'Because, one, there's at least four or five faces looking over here trying to catch a whisper of anything. Two, that should be

167

done in private anyway. I think that's the way we do it. Three, why are you asking me? Why are you not asking Seoras?' Hope emphasised the first name. If he was going to complain about Ross, he'd have it handed right back to him.

'You're right. Of course, you're right, Sergeant. You're very good at this, aren't you? I can see why he has you as a second. Come up and see me when you finish your dinner. Shall we say quarter past?'

That gives me five minutes to finish, thought Hope.

'I think we'll say twenty-five past, if that's okay by you, Alan.'

Hope did not enjoy the next fifteen minutes of dinner. She'd finished within five and sat playing with her diet cola until she eventually drank a large gulp, washed down whatever remained in her mouth, and took the stairs up to the DCI's office.

Hope knocked the door, got a 'come in', and approached a large desk bigger than Macleod's. On the far wall was a large photograph of Alan Lawson, a woman, presumably his wife, and three rather splendid-looking kids. Each one of them was smiling without a hair out of place. Hope found it strange. Why did everybody want to have perfect families? Why do people not want to have a family that was different? A family that stood out, a family that just was and wasn't bothered about what anybody else thought of them.

She had never been just ordinary, but then again, neither had her family. Mum was an old hippie child, so was her father, back to the streets of Glasgow after they needed to actually earn some money instead of just living the dream. And she had learnt that side of life. They were pretty disgusted when she became a police officer, but Hope liked it. This balance she had between the formality and the sense of duty while being able to occasionally just live out a wild existence.

She found John like that as well. He appeared to be this rather dapper man hiring you a car. If you got behind the façade, he was a cavalier and he wanted some fun. No wonder they suited each other so well. Hope turned to see Alan Lawson behind his desk, and he held a hand up while he was on the phone. She stood patiently trying not to move her feet too much as if she was impatient. This was the boss's boss, after all.

'Ah, Sergeant, my apologies,' said Lawson, putting the phone down. 'I'm afraid that was the assistant chief constable wanting to know how we were getting on. I told him we're progressing well. Hopefully, we might have an arrest soon.'

'Where's that coming from?' asked Hope.

'I hoped you would tell me. As I said, I want to know what Macleod is thinking. You see, the public are fearful at the moment. They know these children have been murdered. They know we've got this possible sex attacker on the loose. Well, not anymore. We've got him downstairs.'

'Sex attacker?' queried Hope. 'That's a rather loose way of describing him.'

'Well, how would you describe him?'

'A man with deep sexual issues, struggling to control them, but not someone violent, not someone who's attacked anyone.'

'As far as we know.'

'Indeed,' said Hope, 'as far as we know, but that's not why you called me here.'

'No, no,' said the man. 'Please take a seat.' He pointed to a rather luxurious chair on the other side of the table, but Hope shook her head.

'I prefer to stand. We're not going to be long, are we?'

'I was hoping you would be a little bit warmer than that,' said

Lawson. 'As I said, I was hoping to know Macleod's thinking. How is he seeing Ian Lamb? What does he think of him?'

'I thought the inspector made that quite clear.'

'Is he just teasing him though? Is he just baiting him, when he's in the interview room?'

'No,' said Hope. 'If you want to know exactly what he thinks, why don't you ask him? I'm not sure it's wholly appropriate you're asking me. You want to talk to me about me? Fine, but you're asking me about what's happening in an investigation and bypassing your lead investigator to do it. That's not right.'

'He's quite moral, Macleod, isn't he?'

'Yes,' said Hope. 'He is. He has his standards.'

'I'm not sure what you mean by that.'

'Macleod will do as Macleod sees fit. I understand, Chief Inspector Lawson, that you have got a lot of pressure from up above. I've never really had that much, maybe once. Seoras generally lets us work quite freely. He takes all that flack up above, but understand one thing, he's wholly on the side of getting to find out who this killer is, and he will not stop until he does. At the moment, we're struggling for evidence; we're struggling for anything. Personally, I think he's right with what he says, multiple killers. I think he's right that it's not Ian Lamb. I'd be very surprised if it is. He's got a few more years on me. You learn to listen to him.'

'So, you don't think Macleod thinks that Ian Lamb is guilty?'

'If Seoras thought Ian Lamb was the murderer, he'd have acted straight away after that first death. He wouldn't have hesitated, and if he couldn't find some excuse to arrest him, some excuse to bring him in, he'd have worked something. He certainly wouldn't have let him get out of his sight. He would have put a tail on him, even if he had to do it on the quiet, even if he had to do it himself.'

There came a knock at the door and Lawson shouted for them to wait a minute. 'I'm sure this'll be no one,' he said to Hope, and then walked over to the door, pulling it open. Macleod was standing there. Hope saw him look over at her, somewhat bemused. Then he looked at Lawson. Lawson was smiling, almost as if he was happy that Macleod had walked in. Hope turned away and looked at the picture on the wall, the happy, smiling family. So perfect. She didn't know the DCI, but she was beginning to feel that she might start to understand him.

'Oh, you're in here, Hope. Okay,' said Macleod. 'I just wanted to come up and speak to the DCI.'

'Alan. I keep telling you it's Alan, Seoras, but it's okay. You can speak in front of Hope. I take it, it's nothing personal.'

'No,' said Macleod. 'I just want to know when we're going to release Lamb.'

'Why would we release Lamb? Lamb shows that we're doing something. Lamb shows that we're on the case at the moment. You've given me nothing else.'

'But Lamb's not the person we're looking for.'

'There's two things here, Seoras. There's the case and getting to the end of it, and there's the management of public opinion in the interim. I know that you can work the case. However, I'm not always convinced that you've managed public expectations.'

Hope thought this was funny. It wasn't that long ago they wanted to run Macleod on a public campaign to restore calm amongst warring neighbourhoods.

'Forget the public,' said Macleod. 'Don't do this to this man. He needs to be let out. He needs to be released. He's not guilty. He's not our murderer. You can call him guilty of being a pervert if you want; you can call him a man of issues, get him treatment for that, but he's not a killer and, therefore, we shouldn't be holding him. When can I release him?'

'Okay, Inspector,' said Lawson. 'If that's what you really want to do, you can release him. But trust me, it's not going to go well.'

'I don't do things because they go well,' said Macleod. 'I do them because it's the right thing to do. Anyway, back to work. Are you coming, Hope?'

'I was just going to take a few more moments of the sergeant's time,' said Lawson.

'I don't think so,' said Hope. 'I think we're done.' With that, she turned on her heel and left the room.

Chapter 21

Clarissa Urquhart looked at the faces in front of her and gave her head a sad shake. She reached for a cup, taking it to her mouth, tilting it up and then finding the mere dribble of coffee arrived. This was her third time through, looking at the books; third time of peering over and over again at faces she didn't know. Every face looked back with that sombre, *you've-just-been-arrested* look. Don't smile too much, just face the front. Turn this way, turn that way. None of them a picture of joy, and Clarissa was sure she was having no joy either.

It couldn't have been her, could it? It couldn't have been her mind. She knew she was getting older, but seriously, was she really at such a level that she couldn't recall the faces she'd seen, all three of them? Forbes, she remembered, but they knew who he was. She'd been there, talked to him, got absolutely nothing from him, and if he was a man running some sort of dodgy cult, then he was hardly going to welcome her, was he?

Clarissa stood up and gave herself a little shake because she had started to feel cold. The offices were never cold at night in the station, but she found more and more as she got older, she felt cold, or it was the medication she took that was doing it.

173

Sometimes she thought about not taking the medication, but that was the problem, wasn't it? If she didn't take it, it might end up rather badly, so it was always safer to take it, just in case. But then you had to put up with the cold.

She wandered over to the coffee machine on the edge of the office and poured herself a cup. As ever, it was topped up, for Ross seemed to appear the minute it ran out, to put a fresh batch on. It was like the man was some sort of inhuman waiter knowing what you needed before you even began, but she wasn't complaining. All was good and it was nice having the younger man about. He was quite a breath of fresh air, especially beside stoic Macleod.

She could have banter with Ross, have a bit of fun with him, in a way she never felt quite secure with Hope. Macleod was the obvious one to take serious heed of as the boss but Hope and she were on a level. Well, Hope was slightly above, she had the final word. Still, she'd been sent off to find out about the knife, but she also wanted to find out about the men in the group. Could she track them down first? Before she resolved to head off and get deeper into the art world with the knife, she thought she'd spend the evening going through the books, all the photos of people previously detained.

'Any luck?'

It was Ross, marching into the room as if it was a summer's day and they weren't in the middle of a rather depressing and serious investigation.

'No,' said Clarissa, 'Nothing. I've been through these things three times. At the moment, I'm struggling to see faces. Never mind trying to identify them properly.'

'Yes, maybe that's the problem. Maybe they're not there,' said Ross.

'Do you think?' said Clarissa. 'Thanks for that.'

'No. No, you don't get me,' said Ross. 'Maybe they're not there. Maybe that's the wrong place to look because these aren't people who've done this before.'

'What are you getting at?' asked Clarissa.

'Well, think about it. The boss has got this idea that it's three different people. One's not done it as well as the other two. You're at that meeting, he said that somebody was leaving the group. Well, maybe they haven't done this before.'

'They don't leave any DNA. Don't leave any—'

'No, they don't, do they? Well-trained then. You know when you do police training, some of us actually get it right the first time. Screw it up the second, the third, maybe fourth, or some other time down the line, but we get trained to do something, we do it right quite often the first time, paying attention.'

'So, you're telling me I've just wasted my time looking through these books?'

'Well, I don't know,' said Ross, 'do I? But maybe you want to look in other places.'

'Like where?'

'Well, think about it. You've got all this symbology. It's coming from different parts of the world; there's nothing to say it's from a particular culture, but it's all about death. Maybe you need to be looking at occultic places, low-level occultic magazines, and interest groups.'

'They're not going to talk about that sort thing in a magazine, are they?'

'Of course not,' said Ross. 'That's not the point, but these people that are involved, you know murderers don't just have an interest in murders, they have other interests. Sometimes they filter in, don't they? Sometimes there's a link, especially in this one, I would think, because you've got all this symbology and joining an actual group. If it is some ritual thing, or supposed ritual thing, then well, this would be a hobby gone across.'

'A hobby?' queried Clarissa. She took the coffee to her lips and began to drink. When she next set it down, she looked back at him. 'I wouldn't call it a hobby, but you could be onto something else. You could be. The knife, it's almost like some Hammer horror film, isn't it?'

'A what horror film?'

'Hammer horror film,' said Clarissa. 'Like the really old horror films they used to do, used to have all those famous people in it. Peter Cushing and that.'

'I saw Dracula. It wasn't him. Gary Oldman.'

'You're a child,' said Clarissa, 'aren't you? God loves you. You're just a child, but you're not a stupid one. Only thing is, Ross, where do I find these low-level occultic magazines?'

'Well, you're going to want something Scottish based, don't you? It's unlikely if they're going to feature, they're going to be featuring in something major, national, or international. They're going to be in something much more low-level, much more local. Let's have a look.'

Clarissa stood behind Ross as he delved into the internet. Very soon, he'd drawn up a list of links for her to look through, magazines that didn't look dodgy, but just were dealing with very weird concepts and not run-of-the-mill occurrences.

'And so what? I just flick through these?'

'Look for the photos. See if you can find any local people writing in or whatever. Or maybe they're featured in club news or whatever. That's what you need to be looking at,' said Ross. 'You might find them there. Things they wouldn't even think twice about being in because they're not dodgy, they're not weird, they're not . . . well, they are weird, but they're not criminal. They don't say, look at us, we murder people, we're after kids.' His voice slowed down somewhat, and he went quiet.

'Are you okay?' asked Clarissa.

'No,' said Ross, 'I've dealt with the death of children before, murder,' he said, 'but it was different then. I wasn't looking to have one of my own. It just feels different.'

'I don't know,' said Clarissa, 'I've never entertained the possibility or thought.'

'Never?'

'No, I couldn't,' said Clarissa.

Ross put his head down but mused, 'Never thought about adoption or that?'

'Got into the business career, just took off. I just never got round to it. I'm probably too selfish to have kids,' she said.

'You probably are.'

Clarissa took a step back. 'What?'

'You probably are,' said Ross, 'I mean, you are quite self-focused. I don't mean that as a bad thing; it's just the way you are.'

'Well, that's pretty frank,' she said. 'Thanks, Job's comforter. Thanks for building me up with that one.'

'I didn't mean any . . .'

'I know you didn't,' she said, 'I know and you're probably right, though. I probably am too selfish. I need to get down to it and look at these delightful magazines you've put in front of me. It's a good job everything's on the internet these days, isn't it?' she said. 'It would probably take a few weeks to collect all these magazines up if we went local.'

'Without doubt, although you probably would've been at the library. I'm sure they have most of them.'

Clarissa settled down with a cup of coffee and began running through the links put up in front of her. She scrolled through page after page intending to look at the photographs because it was late, but every now and again, she read an article.

There are some weirdos in this life, she said to herself. *Who in their right mind dresses up like that?* She was looking at a man with a large robe on and some antlers coming out of his head. He had himself down as some grand wizard and she found it hard not to just laugh. The man must have been nearly sixty-five. Around him were a number of women wearing white robes described as young virgins. Some of them looked older than her. A lot of it was all a game.

The more she read, the more she realised that this was just people playing, just having a bit of fun. She read another magazine, which seemed to put the blame for everything on a shift in the stars, talking about things rising from the depths. Again, she was amazed at what people would swallow, what fantasy would take their minds. Unless, of course, they thought it wasn't fantasy. Or was this just all a bit of a laugh?

Maybe it was. Maybe she should get into one of these things. Although she wasn't going to wear any antlers on her head and there was no way they were going to dress her up in white as a virgin. Clarissa saw Ross look over a few times, catching her laughing, but then she saw something, a face. A face from a bookshop.

She started to read the article about a bookshop in the borders, which sold rare books. There was a new occultic section, apparently having older books, which were spell books and other things detailing witches' Sabbaths, and other such delights. Some of the words Clarissa didn't even understand.

Clarissa blew up the face from the article, so it filled her entire screen and then looked vaguely disappointed because it was heavily pixelated. She made it smaller but finally, she admitted she was struggling. She thought it was the face, but she couldn't be sure. She called Ross over.

'Can you make this bigger, make it so it actually looks proper, not just all sorts of dots?'

'Of course,' said Ross, 'it's not difficult if you just . . .'

'Don't tell me; just do it for me. Some of us are too old to learn.'

'Don't want to, more like; you want to have the young lad do it for you.' She looked up, thinking he was offended, but he was smiling broadly. 'You're not the only one who can tease. Either way, watch this.'

'That's him, that's him,' she said.

'Well, that's something,' said Ross. 'We're going the right direction with this. Let's see who he is.'

The man in the article was described as a rare book collector who had opened up this bookshop quite recently. Clarissa checked the article's date. That was, at least, two years ago. She wondered if it was still there. Ross delved into the business address book and came back showing an address for the Arnold's Rare and Occultic Book House, located in the Scottish borders. Clarissa reckoned that was a good five-hour drive, at least. She checked her watch; it was one in the morning.

'What do I do?' she said to Ross. 'Jump in the car and drive through the night to get there?'

'On your own, that's not a good idea, is it?'

'No, but it's this case, isn't it? You feel like you need to do everything now. Need to do it before . . .'

'Before it happens to some other poor kid. Yes, I get it,' said Ross, 'but it's not going to do you good if you don't get any sleep. I mean, how much have you had over the last couple of nights?'

'Not an awful lot, more than the boss, still.' She looked over her shoulder, saw Macleod's office, his lights still on. He was working away inside, no doubt going over and over the various reports. 'I'm going to tell him I'm heading off down,' she said.

'Just be careful,' said Ross, 'driving, I mean.'

'Of course,' said Clarissa, 'but I can handle myself in both regards, not just the driving.'

'Of course,' he said.

Clarissa made her way into Macleod's office, not even bothering to knock. It was one in the morning; he should be happy at the visit.

'What is it?' said the decidedly dour inspector from over the table.

'I've got something, Seoras. One of the faces I saw at the meeting, I identified him. He runs a bookstore down in the borders. I'm just about to go.'

This caused Macleod to look up promptly. 'You okay driving down at this time?'

'I'm not part of the OAP section,' she said. 'I can still drive well.'

This was true—she was not an Old Age Pensioner. One thing Clarissa could do was drive. She loved to drive but having a bit of company on the drive wasn't going to go amiss, though.

'Take somebody with you. Find somebody from the night shift who wants a bit of overtime. Bring them back up tomorrow. They can always drive.'

She gave Macleod an intense stare. 'That's my car we're

180

talking about,' said Clarissa. 'I don't have a problem with somebody sitting in it, but they are not driving.'

'Okay,' said Macleod, 'whatever. Take somebody if you want. Let me know in the morning what happens.'

'What are you working on, anyway?' she asked.

'I'm going to release Ian Lamb in the morning, early, to try and get him away before, well, the media scrum.'

'Good luck with that,' said Clarissa. 'I'll give you a buzz when I find anything.'

'Just be careful; this is a murderer we're after.'

'That's different from normal, how?' asked Clarissa. 'Just because it's kids, it doesn't make it different.'

'Oh, it does,' said Macleod, 'and you know it does.'

'Yes,' she said, 'I do.'

Clarissa walked out of the office and went over to where her shawl was hanging from the coat rack. She threw it on and was about to turn to walk out the door when there was a shout from Ross. She turned and saw one of the hot cups, the thermally insulated ones that they kept around the office. He was holding it up to her, along with a smile.

'Caffeinated, ready to go.'

She walked up to him, put her arms around him, and gave him a hug. Macleod was right; these cases did feel different. It was good to know people had your back.

Chapter 22

Macleod shook himself as he woke with a start. He checked his watch—six in the morning. They were due to let Ian Lamb out in an hour's time, so he'd better get along and smarten himself up. He was worried that there could be press there and he certainly didn't want to look like the dishevelled wreck he did at the moment.

He'd slept fitfully in the chair, not for long enough anyway, sometime after three. At some point soon, he'd have to sleep properly, have to take a good eight hours out and find a bed back home. He just wanted something to go on. Clarissa was chasing, but it wasn't anything unique, anything that had a great feel to it.

They'd spoken to Jona and the DNA chase was nowhere. They'd come up with no DNA on Sandy Mackay other than her own. Surely if someone had gone to bed with her . . . but then again, Sandy couldn't remember much. She allowed them to conduct an examination and Jona said that she'd certainly had sex with someone the previous night. At the very least, if they could identify them, it would bring them into question. Whether or not he was actually the killer would not be proven by a DNA find alone.

Jona was bemused, though. She said that if they'd had sex, then she really would've been able to identify the person. She understood the other crime scenes. She understood that at times people could work in a way to operate clean, but not when you take someone to bed. It wasn't like she'd been murdered and then they managed to clean up. It was almost too much to think about at the moment. Macleod was struggling on that front.

He roused himself, walked over to the far side of his office where he opened up a wardrobe and found three new shirts hanging there. Jane had been in. Been in and not even said hello. She must have seen him sleeping. Either that or she'd dropped them in at the door and some wise constable had decided not to wake him. Maybe it was Ross. Macleod looked to the outside office and there was Ross behind his computer.

Macleod went down to the showers, stood under one for ten minutes before then cleaning himself thoroughly. When he came back up to the office, he looked like an exhausted man in a rather clean suit.

'Coffee, sir?' said Ross, approaching with a cup. Macleod thanked him. 'Do you want me to pop down and get you some breakfast from the canteen? Maybe a croissant or something? Bit of a pick-me-up before you do this?'

'Yes,' said Macleod. 'That would be good.' Five minutes later Macleod was sitting, eating a croissant, and sipping his coffee. He was almost finished when the phone rang.

'DI Macleod?'

'It's Alan upstairs,' said the DCI. 'Are you sure you want to do this? I still think it's unwise.'

'He's an innocent man. Well, innocent of murder,' said Macleod. 'There's no point in holding him. He needs to be out of the public eye because these things can get nasty.'

'I think they already have. I take it you haven't seen the protest out on the street.'

Macleod looked to his window. He didn't face the exit of the police station and he had to put his face right up against the window and peer round. It was then he saw the cameras and the crowd and drew himself away from the window with dispatch.

'When did they come here?' asked Macleod. 'How did they know?'

'Might be better to hold onto him.'

'And do what?' asked Macleod. 'Leave it so we have a siege-like situation?'

'It's out on the news. Everything about him, where he lived and the flat upstairs,' said the DCI. 'That crowd thinks he did it. They're letting people know.'

'Crowd can think whatever they want. I'm running an investigation here, not a popularity contest,' said Macleod. 'Who did that? Who let this slip? I'm going to go through them.'

'It happens, Macleod. It happens more often than you know.'

Macleod thought for a minute. *I've run more investigations than this guy, probably.* 'What on earth are you talking about? It doesn't happen on my watch,' said Macleod. 'It doesn't happen on my watch.'

He stood up as Hope came through the door of his office and he waved her over to a seat while he continued on the phone with the DCI.

'We still go ahead. We get him out, put a blanket over his head, run him out in a police van. Take him elsewhere and drop him or else get him back to his house. See what he wants to do. He may want to go somewhere else.'

'Very good,' said the man. 'It's up to yourself. I'm advising against this, but, and I'm fair, I'll let you run the investigation.'

Macleod couldn't help but feel that was a loaded conceit, but he said a very straightforward 'thank you' before he placed the phone down and looked over at Hope, his eyes full of anger.

'Somebody's gone and dropped the ball on this one. Some-body's gone and told them.'

'Who? Who told who what?' said Hope. She'd been at home for a couple of hours, resting, Macleod's plan to try and rotate the troops. He knew it was always good for Hope to be rested in case she had to take over from him at any point.

'Somebody's told the press about Ian Lamb's possible in-volvement. They know about upstairs in the flat, all about that and they know he's getting out very shortly.'

'Yes, I saw them outside. On the telly, they've practically condemned him,' said Hope.

'But he's not involved. He's not involved,' said Macleod, raising his voice.

'Easy,' said Hope. 'I know that. You know that.'

'Well, find out who's feeding these people this information. Find out who's dropping him in it. I don't like this. I really don't like this. We've got a murderer on the loose, several of them, probably, and all we're getting is somebody holding up a token figure, somebody for appeasement.'

'Well, if you keep him in the cells, they'll soon find out it's not him when the next one dies.'

'We don't want the next one to die,' said Macleod, his voice suddenly hoarse.

'You're talking to me,' said Hope. 'You're talking to me. You know as well as I do, I'm the next person behind you in wanting to stop these killings.'

Macleod turned away. He walked towards the window and then he stepped back from it. 'Press,' he said. 'Always press around, getting in the way.'

'Do you want me to take Lamb out? I don't mind. I can do it.'

'No,' said Macleod. 'That wouldn't look good, would it? Complaining about this guy being taken out and the lead investigator's not there to stand by his decision, sent out his woman.'

'His what?' said Hope.

'His woman. That's what they called you. I heard it the other day.'

'The news?'

'No, talk radio program. Was on in the car. Price of celebrity, eh? I always get called Macleod. You never get Sergeant McGrath, you get Macleod's woman or the lovely McGrath, the lovely Hope, the redheaded bombshell detective.'

'They say that about me? Really?'

'You've not heard it? You must have heard it at some point. The lower, gutter ones, not the proper news reports.'

'No. I don't listen to them. I don't read them, ignore them completely because this is what they do to you to wind you up. I fought hard to be in this position. I don't need some hack telling me I got there because of my sexuality.'

'You didn't, you know that, don't you,' said Macleod suddenly.

'Seoras, get a hold of yourself,' said Hope. 'Of course, I know it. What's bugging you? No, don't tell me. I know what's bugging you. We're not making any progress. We're not getting anywhere. Where's Clarissa?'

'She's gone down to the borders. She saw a face in a magazine, one that she said was a face she saw in the upstairs building. She's chasing him down, probably there, actually. Drove through the night.'

'I take it you sent somebody with her,' said Hope.

'Left it as her choice. Offered.'

'We're dealing with a murderer here. You sure she should be running off down there on her own?'

'This is Clarissa,' said Macleod. 'She's not daft. She won't take risks.'

'She took a risk climbing up on those roofs. She can't walk properly at the moment; she's got a sore foot. She's affected by this case, same as you, same as us all. Only she's at a point where she's stretching beyond what she should do.'

'Yes, she is.'

'She wants to please you,' said Hope. 'You get that about her, don't you? You get that the one thing she'll do is try to impress you with what she's doing.'

'She's a good police officer. She knows how to work. She can take care of herself.'

'She's not blind, though. She's seeing what this is doing to you; she's seeing what it's doing to the rest of us. She wants it finished so she will push harder than normal. That's how she hurt her leg.'

'Well, maybe we all need to push a bit harder,' said Macleod.

'What's that meant to mean?' said Hope.

'Nothing. Means nothing. Come on, let's go get this done.'

Macleod stormed off out through the office and Hope followed him a few paces behind. He knew he was being moody, knew that he was reacting harshly, but that's why Hope was there. There to check him, there to step in if he made any

187

mistakes. She was good like that, and yes, he did know deep down that Hope wouldn't do anything just to impress him. Clarissa might, he was aware of that. She just might.

Macleod walked down to the cells where Ian Lamb was being booked out. Macleod checked what Lamb had wanted and was advised by an officer that he'd be taken into a van with a blanket over his head and they would take him back to his house, again, running him inside.

'He does know that he's going to be covered off. Press media everywhere.'

'Yes, he does,' said the officer. 'I've taken him through it several times. He thinks it's for the best.'

The DCI appeared and strode up to Macleod, once again asking him the same question.

'Are you sure you want to do this, Seoras? Are you sure you want him out?'

'Out?' seethed Macleod. 'He's hardly going to be out, is he? We're putting him in a van; he's going to his house. Press are all over him, now probably watching him closer than we can in that cell in here.'

'Okay,' said the DCI. Ian Lamb was brought out and Macleod walked with him to the rear doors of the station. There was a clamouring outside of press and they could hear chants of 'child killer, child killer.'

'Are you okay, Mr Lamb?' asked Macleod.

'You do believe that I didn't do it, don't you?' he said. 'I know I'm not perfect, but I didn't do this. I didn't do . . .'

'I know you didn't,' said Macleod. 'That's why you're going out those doors. If I thought you did, you wouldn't be leaving that cell.'

'Thank you,' he said, 'thank you,' and Macleod saw a man

who was desperate for someone to believe in him. An officer came up with a blanket and they draped it over Lamb and two officers went side by side with him and a number went out in front. Macleod watched as the police van was driven up. Quickly, the door was opened and they pushed out through the press scrum.

'Is this our killer, Macleod? Is this our killer?' Macleod put his hand up, issuing the simple rebuff of, 'No comment.' For a moment their small party's progress was impeded and then a hand went up, pulling back the blanket that was over Lamb. He looked up. The flashes went off.

'Clear the way,' said Macleod. 'You, back. Clear the way.' He heard Hope shouting behind him as well and slowly they managed to get Ian Lamb into the van before slamming the door behind him. It sped off with newspaper men running after it. Macleod turned around to see the DCI being accosted.

'Detective Chief Inspector, do you agree with this decision? Are you happy that the murderer has been let loose?'

Macleod looked and waited for the standard comment to come back, but instead the DCI tried to make himself as tall as possible, his short stature barely rising above the cameras around him.

'Our lead investigator's decided that Mr Lamb has nothing to answer for at this time. Thereby we have duly set Mr Lamb free.'

Macleod watched as the cameras turned to him. 'Is that right? Have you decided that he should go?'

Inside Macleod was seething. The DCI had thrown the decision onto him, had shown that he was the one responsible for it. You didn't do that. You backed your people. The DCI was making sure that if this went wrong, Macleod would get

189

hung for it.

'Detective Inspector Macleod, are you convinced that Ian Lamb is not the killer?'

Macleod snapped. 'I've just released him; what do you think?' With that he stormed off inside, knowing he'd just let the press get the better of him.

Chapter 23

Clarissa yawned as the small green sports car trundled into the tiny Scottish village of Tavish in the borders. Like many border towns, Tavish consisted of a long main street with a couple of shorter streets running off it. There was a new housing estate, some distance away as well as some older farmhouses making it a mini-hub for the local area. Surrounding Tavish were plenty of fields which Clarissa had enjoyed as she drove the car this way and that through the winding roads before arriving in the sunlit village.

As she stepped out of the car, she felt the chill. Despite this and the fatigue she felt, having driven down through most of the night, she was in a good mood. She was on the case. She'd also had two hours sleep when she'd felt so tired that she pulled the car over and simply napped in it. The cold had woken her up because despite having the hood up, there wasn't much heat to be found within the sports car. Now that she had shaken off the cobwebs of the last couple of hours driving, she looked around for anywhere that might sell coffee at this hour.

It was eight o'clock in the morning and nowhere was really open. She located a small supermarket and made do with one of those machines that dispensed coffee. Macleod would've been angry with her, describing it as 'that muck'. At this hour of the morning, and with the departing coffee from Ross long gone, she needed something to keep her awake.

Marching along the main street, taking copious sips of the coffee, Clarissa looked to locate the small bookshop that was her target. When she reached it, she was totally underwhelmed. There was a small front of a window, which displayed about seven or eight books in it on tiny wooden stands. The display was unimpressive, and the book titles meant nothing to her. Beside the window, there was a small door with a glass front and a sign saying 'open'.

She tried the door, finding it was locked. As she looked deeper inside, she saw no lights were on. Clarissa thought she should take a look around the back just in case someone was still about and so wandered on down the street until she found an alley that went round to the rear. She counted the building numbers until she found what she thought was the correct rear entry.

Clarissa pushed at the wooden gate which was over a person high, but found again, it was locked. She tried to jump up to put her hands on the wall above it, but when she found out she couldn't hold on very well and kept landing on her good foot, she decided not to try for a proper grab in case she fell back down on her extremely sore ankle.

Okay, she thought, *what to do?* Marching back around to the front of the buildings, she found that the butcher shop next door to the bookshop had lights on inside. She approached the front door, banging on it, and found it wasn't open. An older man in the back looked at her and shouted something about nine o'clock. Clarissa took out her warrant card and slapped it up on the window and the man raced forward. He opened up, apologising profusely.

'I'm sorry. I didn't realise. What's happened, what's gone wrong? Is somebody hurt out there?'

'No,' said Clarissa. 'Nobody's hurt.' And she limped into the shop.

'Have you hurt yourself?' asked the man.

'Yes,' said Clarissa. 'I have but not here. That was back up in Inverness. No, I wanted to ask you about next door.'

'Next door,' said the man. 'Which side?'

'The bookstore next door. I've come down to try and see the man who works there. Winston Arnold, that's his name, isn't it?'

'Winston, yes, that's Winston. He's a nice enough man. What do you want with Winston?'

'To be honest sir, that's really my business. I was just wanted to know, have you seen him lately?'

'Oh, of course. Sorry. I shouldn't be asking like that, should I?' The man was probably in his late sixties and had a very gentle way about him. His greying hair covered most of his head and he was clean-shaven, but he had the shoulders and arms of a butcher through years of cutting meat and hefting large pieces about.

'I haven't seen Winston since . . . oh, when was it? Yesterday morning. I came back yesterday morning, and I noticed that the shop was shut up. Well, I say shut up. The lights were off yesterday afternoon. There's still an open sign up, isn't there?'

'Yes, there is,' said Clarissa. 'I noticed that. Is that normal?'

'No,' said the man. 'It's not normal. He normally turns it over for closed and what I thought was he'd made a mistake or something. I was wondering maybe he had a family emergency or that.'

'Does he have any family?'

'Not that I know of. I meant far away. Maybe a sister or something.'

'How well do you know Winston?'

'Not very. He said he had a trip up to Inverness recently. I only know that because I met him, and he said he was up on some business. Well, he's a bookman, isn't he? Maybe there's those fairs and that. He does that quite often. Limps off to find old books at good prices. Can't blame him for that, can you?'

'I guess not,' said Clarissa. 'Strange books though, aren't they?'

'Oh, he is into all that weird stuff. I'll give you that.'

'Does he ever talk about it with you?'

'He tried once,' said the man. 'He was telling me he had a copy of something or other, sixteenth century, he said or maybe that's not right. Maybe it was nineteenth or eighteenth. I don't know. Anyway, the name of it was in French and I had no idea what he was talking about. It's like when I talked to him about a good side of beef, man's clueless. Absolutely clueless. He came in one day for pork, a bit of pork belly. In fact, he didn't come in for it. He came in and asked what he should cook. I asked him how many and I suggested a bit of pork belly. I said to him, "Do you want that scored?" He just looked at me. Why would you want to do that? You score it for the crackling, don't you? It makes great crackling if you score it properly. Get the salt in.'

'Yes, it does,' said Carissa. 'Do you know anything beyond that, where he lives or that?'

'Lives above the shop,' said the butcher. 'That's what he does.

He came down here, oh, not that long ago. Couple of years moved in, and he's been fine as a neighbour. You haven't got a clue what goes on behind closed doors, but there's no harm from him. No harm at all. Races off here and there to go to whatever meetings.'

'What meetings are these?'

'I have no idea. I think they must be something to do with the books, like I say, but he's not been a bother. None at all.'

'Thank you. If you hear from him, can you contact me?' asked Clarissa, handing the man a card.

'Oh, will do. Get him to phone you if you want.'

'That'd be good,' said Clarissa, 'but you make sure you contact me as well, just to be sure in case he forgets.'

'Will do. Do you want anything before you go?'

'What?' asked Clarissa.

'You people, you're running around so much. I just wondered if you wanted to pick up something for your dinner before you went. It's all right. I won't tell your boss.'

Clarissa almost laughed. The one thing Macleod wouldn't get annoyed about was her picking up a nice piece of steak and that, but she had other things to do, so she thanked the man and stepped outside.

Walking back to the shop next door, she looked in the window, peering to see if anything was amiss, but there was nothing. She looked through the glass of the door. On a mat was an opened envelope, like somebody had just dropped it. Beside the envelope, was a letter.

She thought about breaking in. That wouldn't work, would it? Bad idea. She could go and get permission to enter, but that would take time as well. Besides, she wasn't too sure she would get it. After all, it was pretty flimsy what they were standing on. There was no direct connection into the case, was there? It was a thread they were pulling. To actually be allowed to march into someone's premises and search, you need something a good bit stronger.

She looked up and down the street. There weren't a lot of people about. Clarissa went down on her knees beside the letterbox at the bottom of the door. She slipped her hand in, pulling her top up to her shoulder. She found she could squeeze in up to her elbow and stretch desperately with her fingers, just managing to touch the envelope. She pulled it closer towards her. It caught on the paper of the letter, swinging it around closer as well. Clarissa reached over with her hand further touching down on the paper, just gradually making it slip towards her.

As she got hold of it in her hand, she heard somebody coming down the street. She tried to extract her hand, pulling the arm out, letter in her hand, and slipping it underneath her shawl as footsteps arrived beside her.

'Are you okay, love?' asked a voice.

Clarissa looked up. 'Sorry, shoelace,' she said. 'Just fixing it.'

The man nodded and walked on past. Clarissa stood up and thought about the fact that her shoes had no laces on them. She'd probably best get out of the way in case the man came back.

She hobbled on back to the green sports car and sat down, opened the envelope up and saw a letter which was written in what she thought looked like Latin, but there were also a large number of symbols. She placed the letter down on the seat beside her, took out her phone and began taking photographs. Once she'd finished that, she placed a call on her mobile to Professor Claudia Wisecroft. She answered it in rather startled fashion.

'Hello. You're early.'

Clarissa looked at her watch. It wasn't that far off nine o'clock. 'I need something from you,' said Clarissa. 'I've just acquired a letter with a lot of symbols on it and some Latin. I need you to take a look at it and tell me what it says.'

'Okay, well you could send it through, and I'll get back to you.'

'I was hoping you'd take a look at it while I was on the phone,' said Carissa. 'It could be important.'

'Life and death important?' asked the professor.

'It could be important,' said Clarissa. 'I'd really appreciate if you looked at it now.'

'Okay, then send it through. Here's my link for my messenger.'

Clarissa listened to the woman speak, took down the messenger address and then went into her phone to link it through. Once she'd done so, she sent a message asking if it was the correct one. The professor sent a message back confirming it, and Clarissa sent through all the information she had in picture form.

She sat there with her foot beginning to throb, regretting having used it for driving down through the night, but she was also getting impatient. Surely the woman could read it quicker than this. Her phone rang again.

'Professor.'

'Detective Sergeant, I've had a look. I'll need some more time to look at some of the other symbols, but basically what it's saying is that somebody is leaving the circle. I don't think it's by choice. It looks like a possible ultimatum of sorts. I think it's talking about past transgressions.'

'What do you mean past transgressions?'

'I don't know but somehow, they've offended the group. That's what I'm getting from it.'

'What does the Latin say?'

'It's just basically saying that this is a missive from the group. It's important and you'll follow the actions given below, but frankly, there's no actions that I can understand.'

'What's the overall feel of it though?'

'Like I said, it's somebody being told they're leaving the group. I'm not sure about the way . . . there's obviously symbols of death again, after life in that messed up context, absolutely abused in the way they've presented them, but they're there.'

'Keep working on it,' said Clarissa. 'Keep working on it. Then I'll come back to you. I need to phone the boss.'

She put the phone down, thought about phoning Macleod, but thought it best if she sat down and thought through what she was doing. Her stomach rumbled. Must be a cafe around here, she thought. A cafe to sit down, give the professor an hour or two and then she could call it in. There would always be time for stuff like that.

* * *

There was nothing like a beach clean to get the juices flowing first thing in the morning. She may have been eighty-five, but Clara was going to clean this beach if it was the last thing she did. That was the trouble with Inverness; it had got ridiculous, hadn't it? People just dumped stuff. People just threw the rubbish wherever. Well, she wasn't going to have it. Just because we were down by the bridge, didn't mean that the beaches didn't deserve to be cleaned.

Yes, there weren't great beaches down here, more stones than anything else, but that didn't matter. The place needed to look its part. Clara was good for her age, steady on her feet and she knew it. Her legs may have been thin, but they were legs like an ox had. Strong, stable, and her balance considering her age was good.

She walked over several stones, reached down and picked up an empty condom packet, throwing it in. Why on earth would you have that down here? Next to a cola can was a broken bin. Then there was some more rubbish and a newspaper. Bit by bit, she worked her way down to the shore, and then she saw a pillar that came down from the bridge.

She thought she saw an arm lying just out round the pillar. *Probably somebody drunk,* thought Clara, and she walked carefully over the stones until she got down close. There she was. *Look at that,* she thought. The woman must have been early twenties at best, possibly younger.

She was lying still in a jacket and jeans. Tara reached down, slapping the woman's face, but she wasn't reacting. She was breathing though, and Clara thought she was asleep rather than unconscious. She couldn't be sure though. It was probably going to be best if she called somebody. After all, as fit as she was, she couldn't lift a woman off the beach. Maybe the tide would come up, although she didn't think it reached this high.

Clara looked for watermarks and the seaweed was below her. She was probably okay. She reached down again, tapping the woman's face, but there was no rousing her. It was then she looked across at the pillar beyond. Clara stumbled, and she fell hard with a hand reaching out, and she thought that her wrist cracked as she came down.

She screamed in pain, but she looked up to see what had caused her to fall, that image that had driven into her mind. There was a child standing upright, but with their back to her. The back was bare, the blonde hair rolling down onto the shoulder blades and touching the many symbols carved on the child's back.

Clara screamed, heaving out what she could with her lungs until she ended up breathless, panicking, and in pain with her wrist. She reached down for the mobile phone. She could barely see the screen, no glasses on and she sat typing frustratingly at the screen. Even with the big buttons that came up on it, she was struggling. *9-9-9*, she thought, *9-9-9*. Three times she tried to call it, three times she hit nine and something else, and then she heard it ring.

Which service do you require?

'Help,' shouted Clara. 'Help. Just help.'

Chapter 24

The Kessock Bridge had brought several moments in Macleod's life, which he'd rather hadn't happened. One of the starkest was when a Santa Claus had jumped off to his death in front of Macleod trying to talk the man down. Therefore, the place always held a dark and foreboding memory. The traffic was busy crossing over it as Macleod made the journey over to Kessock and then down to underneath the bridge where the child's body had been found. He was unaware of many of the details, having simply received the call and raced out. He was surprised when he got there to see so many press, but also beyond them, the DCI had already appeared on scene.

'When we get out, Hope,' he said to his sergeant who was driving the car, 'the press will come over to us. Let me deal with them. You get through the cordon and find out what's going on with the DCI. You seem to have better relations with him at the moment than I do anyway. Probably easier if we do that.'

'You sure, Seoras? I can take the press. It's not a problem.'

'Of course, I'm sure. Just do it. Okay?'

'Okay,' said Hope, 'but don't snatch at me. I'm not the enemy here.'

He drew a deep breath. She wasn't, was she? She was never the enemy. Even though in the back of his mind, he still hadn't worked out what she was doing in with the DCI. He wouldn't ask her. To ask her would be to accuse her, better not to say anything, as if nothing was the matter, that he trusted her, and he did. It was just at the moment, so many things were spiralling out of control, so many things. Another murder. Another murder with next to nothing to go on.

Macleod stepped out of the car and was instantly swarmed by press from all sides.

'Do you have a lead, Inspector? Are we to expect more murders? Do you think you failed to stop this one? Is Ian Lamb the murderer?'

Macleod gave the usual response. 'Investigations are underway; we're looking into this fresh incident. All manpower is being focused towards achieving the correct result of arresting our killer'—standard sound bites. Things you could say in any case.

Macleod continued to field the questions as he walked towards the police cordon, but beyond it, he saw Hope beginning to argue with the DCI. It looked like the man was pulling rank on her. She was furious, absolutely furious, and then her head flicked around to look at him. Her face, it was . . . he'd seen Hope struggle before in life, but this looked beyond that. It wasn't just a struggle; it was frustration, anger, as if she didn't know where to go. If things got that much on top of her, she'd speak to him, but she was looking at him as if he was the last person she would speak to, looking to him as if he were the problem.

He watched her stride off, down towards where forensics

were working, and Macleod made the police cordon, glad he had shrugged off the attentions of the press. Before he had gone more than about three feet beyond, though, the DCI walked up to him.

'Detective Inspector Macleod.'

Detective Inspector Macleod—he was talking about being Seoras and Alan previously. This was too formal, even at a crime scene.

'Detective Inspector Macleod, I'm afraid to advise you that you are off the case.'

'What?' blurted Macleod. 'What do you mean, I'm off the case?'

'Exactly what I've told you. We have four dead now. I can't afford to hang back. I can't put my respect for a colleague who clearly is making no headway ahead of getting this job done. I'm coming down to take personal charge of it. You're off the case. I suggest you take a leave of absence. Don't come into the office; we'll contact you at home when we need you.'

'You don't just kick somebody out like that,' said Macleod.

'You don't want to make a scene, not here,' said Lawson. 'You don't want to be at war with me.'

'Well, who do you think did this then?' said Macleod.

'Ian Lamb,' said the man. 'We know it's Ian Lamb. We know. Now go home.'

Macleod stared at the man. Inside, his stomach was churning. He was a mix of anger, a mix of frustration because he couldn't do anything. Not here. *What should he do? Have a screaming match?* The press was behind him.

Lawson looked back up at him. 'I told you, go home. You're off the case, Macleod.' The tone was severe, but what angered Macleod, was the level at which it was spoken, so clearly within earshot of the press, audible enough for them to hear. He turned, walked back through the crowd, which immediately engulfed him.

'Inspector Macleod, is it your fault we have another dead child? Inspector Macleod, why did you let Ian Lamb out? Macleod, how did you get this so wrong? Have you been fired, Macleod?'

Macleod ignored them, but he wanted to reach out and grab each of them around the throat. He wanted to throw them down into the waters of the Moray Firth, forever to be swept out to sea and never seen again. He saw Ross walk past him with a bemused face before Hope called Ross over. Macleod stepped back into the car, realised that Hope had the keys, and walked back over again surrounded by press.

She must have seen, must have known as she ran through the police cordon up to him and handed over the keys. Maybe she wanted to throw her arms around him, tell him it was all right, tell him they'd made a mistake, but they were surrounded by press. At a time when they needed to have an intimate moment as colleagues, one where they could reassure each other, they were exposed to the worst kind of world.

Macleod took the keys, turned, and solemnly walked back through the crowd. He got into the car, started the engine, and there were people behind him. Cameras pressed in. He slammed down the horn, but they didn't move, so he put on the reversing lights, revving the engine to see them scatter. He took his moment, drove backwards, spinning the car around in a neat little three-point turn, and drove out of Kessock.

What did they mean? thought Macleod. *What'd they mean, Ian Lamb did it? Ian Lamb couldn't have done it. Ian Lamb . . .*

He had said not to come in. The DCI had specifically said not to come in, but Macleod knew he had to cover over some thoughts. This was the time to do it as well, for everyone's attention would be down on the poor little thing who had been dispatched.

Ian Lamb couldn't have done it, thought Macleod. *He couldn't have done it*. He walked in through the rear door of Inverness police station, and he could already see the looks from certain constables. Word spread fast in the police force; that was one thing you were sure of. He saw the way they looked at him.

Before, many would've been afraid of him. This was Macleod. They didn't want to disappoint him. He was ferocious. He took on the establishment. His little Rottweiler came out after you and he knew that the team were defensive of him.

He marched up to his office, stepped inside, and sat down in his chair. Why Ian Lamb? Why Ian Lamb? The phone rang on his desk and Macleod picked it up without even thinking, and then breathed a sigh of relief because Jane was on the other end.

'What are they doing, Seoras? They're here. Lots of them are here. They're telling me that you've got it wrong. They're telling me that somebody else is killing these kids, but you missed it. Are you okay? Are you all right?'

'I didn't miss it,' he said quietly. 'They're not seeing it. The DCI sold me out in front of everyone. Sold me out to save his own skin. I didn't miss it.'

'What should I do, Seoras? Are you coming back to the house? They're everywhere here. What should I do?'

'You need to get out,' said Macleod. 'We won't get any peace at the house. Don't say anything. If anybody tries to speak to you and ask you a question, you say no comment. You lock up the house. If need be, get one of the neighbours to help you, but get out of the house. I'll send someone to pick you up. Be ready to go. Pack a bag for about three or five days. I'm not having you sitting in that cauldron.'

'Seoras, are you okay?'

'No, but I need to think. I need to get under this. I need to . . .' He ran out of what he needed to do. The frustration took over.

'Are you crying, Seoras? Seoras, speak to me.'

He put the phone down. Wasn't any good for her to hear him like this. The phone rang back a few minutes later, but he didn't pick up. About five minutes later, having composed himself, Macleod rang the Assistant Chief Constable.

'I can't speak to you, Seoras, sorry. I just can't speak to you at the moment. It's not going to work.'

'I don't want you to speak to me,' he said. 'Jane's up at the house. She's got a bucket load of press around her. Take her to the Aviemore Hotel. It's on the edge up towards the hills. Get somebody to take her there and make sure they're not tailed. Book her in under a false name and tell her I'll join her soon as.'

'Of course,' he said; 'of course, I'll do that. Look, for what it's worth. We all miss things.'

'I didn't miss anything,' said Macleod suddenly. 'I missed nothing. Ian Lamb didn't do this. This is wrong.'

'But Seoras, they just found it. Didn't anyone tell you?'

'No, what do you mean?'

'Uniform today? They stopped Ian Lamb after he was swimming, got a tip-off. He came out of that swimming pool, got changed, walked out of the building, and when they stopped him, they found the key for the locker the knife was in.'

'What? No,' said Macleod. 'No.'

'Yes. I know it's still circumstantial, but it's tilted massively in his favour that he is the murderer. Can't ignore this. With another child dead, well, I'm sorry, Seoras. It doesn't look good. They need to get you out of there. You need to step aside for a while. You need to . . .'

Macleod put the phone down. 'No,' he said. He stood up, picked his coffee cup off the table, and threw it off the wall. It smashed into three different pieces. The last drags of coffee ran down the wall.

'It's not Ian Lamb,' he said. 'It's not Ian Lamb. It can't be Ian Lamb. I looked him in the eye. I spoke to him. It's not him.'

Everything was closing in. He grabbed his coat, wrapped it around him, looked around his office. Did he need anything? No. There was nothing here he needed. Of course, he wouldn't be allowed to speak to Hope. Not meant to talk to Ross either if he was suspended, but he hadn't been, had he? They hadn't formally said anything. All they'd done was told him to go home and not come in. Told him he was off the case. They hadn't said he'd done anything directly wrong. Was it a press exercise? Were they just covering themselves as ever?

Macleod exited the office and walked down the stairs. He saw some of the younger constables stop and stare. A few shook their heads, but one walked up to him, stopped him from moving forward, physically shoved him.

'I knew Amanda and I knew her kid. You let that bastard back out. You let that bastard out to do it again, Macleod.'

'He's innocent,' said Macleod. 'I'm sorry that she suffered. I'm sorry for what happened, but he didn't do it.'

The man shoved Macleod again. He was many years younger than Macleod and there was no way Macleod could stand here and keep being shoved without gradually moving backwards.

'Don't do it, Willie. Don't do it.'

'You bastard, Macleod!'

He didn't even see it coming. Macleod fell down, the punch catching him on the side of the chin. He felt hands reaching down for him as he hit the stairs, but then someone else was there pulling the man away.

'You bastard, Macleod! You got it wrong!'

Nobody picked him up. Nobody stepped towards him. Was he a pariah in his own station? He lay there for at least thirty seconds trying to get his bearings. Slowly, he got back to his feet and staggered down the remaining steps. He checked his chin, but there was no blood. There would be a bruise alright though, but no blood. Macleod put his head down, walked towards the rear door of the police station, and saw the cameras there. He marched out through them, ignoring them completely as the questions piled in again.

Once inside his car, he drove off, ignoring them, heading out towards the A9 in as direct a fashion as he could. As he drove along, his phone began to ring. He closed off a call from Jane. He closed off a call from Hope, and from Ross. They didn't need to get involved at the moment; they needed to look after themselves; they needed to be on the case. Then a call came in from Clarissa. He pulled over and answered it.

'Seoras, how's things.'

'Not good,' he said. 'They've kicked me out, they've arrested Ian Lamb. They found a key for the locker in his swimming bag today, the one that held a knife.'

'Bloody hell,' said Clarissa. 'That's a turn up. What sort of an idiot is he?'

'He's an arrested idiot,' said Macleod. 'They're saying I got it wrong. There's press everywhere. They're saying, I've got it wrong.'

'You don't believe that, do you?' said Clarissa, but Macleod had switched the phone off, started the engine, and was driving to Aviemore. He needed out. He needed a way out. An inferno had built around him, and he knew he couldn't control it.

Chapter 25

Macleod looked out of the hotel window, the same view he'd looked at for two days previous. It wasn't a bad view. Plenty of mountainside, looking majestic in its autumnal greens and browns, and the leaves were falling off the trees. Soon, they'd be sweeping across the paths, covering them and you'd not have to think about muddy feet because of the brown carpet that had been laid down. At any other time in his life, he may have considered this to be worthwhile.

Jane would've. Jane would've loved it but instead she was behind him, her hands on his shoulder. She was worried for him, he knew that, but she kept rubbing his blasted shoulders, kept rubbing them as if that was going to make everything better. *Ian Lamb*, he thought. The name had been on his lips for the last two days. *Ian Lamb couldn't have done it. There's no way Ian Lamb . . .*

Hope had phoned briefly to say she was sorry, to say that she would back him, but he told her no, just to get on with the investigation. Told her she was on the inside, told her to keep telling him what was going on. She said she couldn't, and he realised she must have been on a work phone. She told him that this was it, just a call to say she was sorry and then she wouldn't be allowed to speak to him. Certainly not about the case.

They'd banned him from receiving any more information. The DCI had described him as a loose cannon, one that was distinctly firing off in the wrong direction. Hope said she'd fought for him, offered her resignation, but the DCI wouldn't have it and Macleod told her bluntly to get right back into the investigation. She and Ross were to behave like they would for him. What mattered were these kids, not Macleod. Macleod was irrelevant. She was upset about his good name though, about the fact that he was being set up.

'Maybe,' he said, but again, that didn't matter. What mattered were these children and the fact to him there was still a killer out there.

During the two days there'd been numerous press calling and the staff at the hotel had their work cut out, filtering out the guests from random reporters trying to get close to Macleod. They didn't all know he was there. In fact, many were unsure, but they'd heard rumours. Macleod didn't entertain the rumours. If they came, they'd get a short, sharp shift.

He advised the hotel it was better if they didn't find out he was there. In truth, the manager was very sympathetic, said he knew nothing about cases and that, but he did know about guests and so far, he'd done a reasonably good job.

There was a thump on the door and Macleod knew Jane had jumped, for the hands left his shoulder.

'What on earth's that, Seoras? Who bangs like that?'

Macleod turned and gave a wry smile. 'That's my Rottweiler,' and he walked over to the door, opening it without checking through the peephole to see who it was.

'Let me in quick,' said Clarissa, and she hobbled into the room. Macleod closed the door quickly.

'It took me ages to get them off my tail. They've been following me. I've been at home medically off on leave and they've been following me. Can you believe that?'

'Absolutely,' said Macleod. 'They haven't exactly been leaving us alone either.'

'Of course not.' Clarissa looked over at Jane. 'Are you okay? Are you holding up?'

'Better than him. He won't talk about it to me. Won't say anything.'

'No, he won't,' said Clarissa, 'because he's brooding. He does this on us too. He's trying to solve this. He's trying to solve it instead of using his team, trying to make sure that none of us get touched by this supposed disgrace he's feeling. Isn't that right?'

Macleod stared up at Clarissa. 'You are an old dog, aren't you?' he said.

'Seoras!' said Jane, but Clarissa was laughing.

'Don't worry, it's a compliment of sorts. What do you know, Macleod?' she asked. 'Tell me what you know, and I'll tell you what I know.'

'I know Ian Lamb didn't do it. Why on earth he's got a key in his bag, I don't know. Who in their right mind would walk around with that? Once the knife's been found, you throw that in a river, you make sure it's in the sea somewhere. Somewhere where it's not going to come back to you. Put it in a bag?'

'Hope doesn't understand that.'

'Hope,' said Macleod cautiously. 'She's not allowed to speak to me about the case.'

'No, but they didn't say she couldn't speak to me. I'm still an officer. I'm just off on a bit of leave, try and get this foot better.'

'That's very convincing,' said Jane.

'That's because it's bloody sore,' said Clarissa. 'If it wasn't for this old fart, I'd be having my feet up watching the telly.'

'So, she's wondering why he's got it in a bag that was searched previously, and nothing was ever found,' said Macleod.

'Exactly. She's got Ross going through the reports. All the bag searches were apparently done correctly. As far as he's aware.'

'It's very easy to get paranoid,' said Macleod, 'but this is about me. This is about somebody else taking their chance, or this might be to do with the circle of killers.'

'You're still convinced on that one. It's a circle.'

'What did Jona say about the latest killing?'

'Similar. No DNA. Mother wasn't molested in any way, just knocked out in some fashion. She came to about four hours after we arrived. Heavily sedated up until then. Carving was done elsewhere according to Jona. Done with one of those knives as far as she can tell.'

'The knife, said Macleod, 'the knife. Where did you get with the knife?'

'About as far as I have with Winston Arnold. He's disappeared off the face of the earth. I'm actually bothered for him. I'm not sure he is still alive.'

'What makes you think that?' said Macleod.

'You know why I think that. The message that was in his shop door basically said that he was out of the group. He was being removed for transgressions. They didn't say what but clearly somebody wasn't happy with his actions, so they decided to get rid of him, as far as I can tell. Makes your group theory even more plausible.'

'Yet they're doing it one by one. Why?' asked Macleod. 'Why? I'm hamstrung though. Look at me. I'm hamstrung. I'm hiding away here.'

'You're not hamstrung,' said Clarissa. 'You're not. You're choosing to be, you're choosing to hide. That's not Seoras. When did you choose to hide?'

'He's protecting me,' said Jane. 'Seoras, I'm out of the way. I'm here.'

'But you need someone with you. Need someone to keep them off you,' said Macleod. 'I won't have them do this to you.'

'Do what to me? I'm stuck in a hotel. What's killing me is you. It's you caving in, sitting here.'

'Woman's right,' said Clarissa. 'It's not you. Telling Hope and Ross to get back at it, that's pot calling the kettle black, that is.'

Macleod scowled across at her. 'Not the same,' said Macleod. 'You don't realise what damage these people can do you.'

'I damn well do,' said Clarissa. 'Why do you think I'm here? You don't get how this feels. I shouldn't even have driven down.'

'Where's the letter?' asked Macleod.

'There's a photo of it. Not that's going to do you any good,' said Clarissa, showing her phone. 'I took it to Jona. Jona can't find anything on it except a set of fingerprints. Don't know who it is because Winston Arnold, funnily enough, isn't on file.'

'Okay, so that's a dead end. We've got nothing then. There's nothing coming from the killings. They're being tight around that. Anybody that steps out of line, they're killing them off. We can't get hold of the group. Winston Arnold's missing.

What have we got?'

'I've got an ornate knife that came from somewhere,' said Clarissa. 'An ornate knife.'

'That could have come from anywhere. You said it yourself, these things are usually cash. There's no records, there's no tracing to be done.'

'How the hell do you think we operate in the art world? We don't just sit there ticking through receipts. How would I have worked with that? I'm not Ross. I don't do the computer tracing. You get out there and you shake people down. You cause a bit of mayhem.'

Macleod looked up her. 'No. I can't ask you to. I can't ask you to go out and jeopardise yourself for this, just for me. I'm practically retired anyway.'

'You never told me this,' said Jane. 'You never told me you're retiring. I'd have taken up my hobby, made sure I got out of the house.'

He looked over at her, then embraced her, holding her close. 'You deserve me. You deserve my time. You don't deserve this. This horror, these shambles.'

'When did it become a shambles, Seoras?' asked Clarissa. 'There's no evidence. We're chasing stuff down. You said he's innocent. If you truly believe Ian Lamb is innocent, let's get back out there and fight. Clear his name. Let's find the bastards that did this to these kids. Kids deserve it if nothing else.'

Macleod sat down on the edge of the bed, his head bowed over. 'There's no point,' he said. 'We won't get there. Not at the moment. There's no fight here. Do you get me? No fight at all. It'll probably go to ground anyway. Especially now they've got Lamb arrested. If he goes back inside, they'll just leave it a while. Leave it a while until you can call it a copycat. These people aren't daft. They've left no DNA, they've left nothing. We haven't got a clue how to get into them. If they take Lamb in, he'll get put away and they'll restart it after a year or two and the DCI will be fat, dumb and happy. There's no point. I can't push your career out the door for that. Neither Hope nor Ross. I'll just take the retirement. I'll take the package and go.'

Clarissa's phone rang and she looked at it, aware that this was a bizarre moment to take a phone call, but she saw it was Ross.

'Als, what's up?'

Macleod watched as she took in what was being said, her face a picture of anger, resentment, but right at the end of the call, she simply thanked him.

'You on a work line?'

Clearly, he said yes, for Clarissa's next words were, 'I'm sure Grumpy's aware.'

Macleod looked up at her. 'Seoras. Ian Lamb killed himself in his cell. I doubt they stopped him. I doubt they even tried.'

'Killed himself. Are we sure? Are we sure somebody didn't dispatch him, called it suicide?'

'Of course, I'm not sure,' said Clarissa.

Macleod walked over to his table, pouring himself a glass of water, drank it quickly, put it down, and stared at Clarissa. 'Too much. Too much. This isn't going to be the end of it. It'll die away for a bit, but it won't be the end of it. They'll be back and there's no way to prove it was them the first time around. He'll have taken the guilt; he'll have taken it all for them.'

'Well, if that's the case, what are we going to do about it?'

Macleod looked up from the bed he was sitting on and saw her face. It was angry, but it was alive. His Rottweiler was spitting, ready to tear at flesh.

'What are we going to do about it, Seoras?'
Slowly, the inspector smiled.

Read on to discover the Patrick Smythe series!

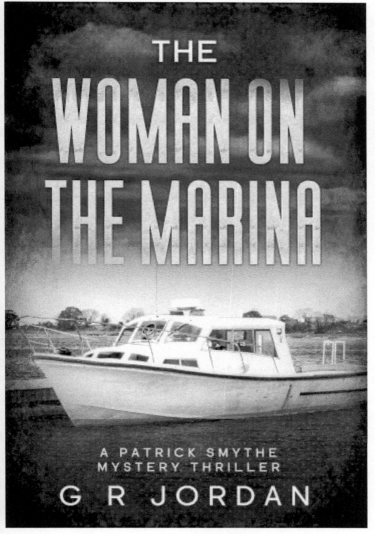

Start your Patrick Smythe journey here!

Patrick Smythe is a former Northern Irish policeman who

after suffering an amputation after a bomb blast, takes to the sea between the west coast of Scotland and his homeland to ply his trade as a private investigator. Join Paddy as he tries to work to his own ethics while knowing how to bend the rules he once enforced. Working from his beloved motorboat 'Craigantlet', Paddy decides to rescue a drug mule in this short story from the pen of G R Jordan.

Join G R Jordan's monthly newsletter about forthcoming releases and special writings for his tribe of avid readers and then receive your free Patrick Smythe short story.

Go to https://bit.ly/PatrickSmythe for your Patrick Smythe journey to start!

About the Author

GR Jordan is a self-published author who finally decided at forty that in order to have an enjoyable lifestyle, his creative beast within would have to be unleashed. His books mirror that conflict in life where acts of decency contend with self-promotion, goodness stares in horror at evil, and kindness blindsides us when we at our worst. Corrupting our world with his parade of wondrous and horrific characters, he highlights everyday tensions with fresh eyes whilst taking his methodical, intelligent mainstays on a roller-coaster ride of dilemmas, all the while suffering the banter of their provocative sidekicks.

A graduate of Loughborough University where he masqueraded as a chemical engineer but ultimately played American football, Gary had worked at changing the shape of cereal flakes and pulled a pallet truck for a living. Watching vegetables freeze at -40'C was another career highlight and he was also one of the Scottish Highlands "blind" air traffic controllers.

These days he has graduated to answering a telephone to people in trouble before telephoning other people to sort it out.

Having flirted with most places in the UK, he is now based in the Isle of Lewis in Scotland where his free time is spent between raising a young family with his wife, writing, figuring out how to work a loom and caring for a small flock of chickens. Luckily, his writing is influenced by his varied work and life experience as the chickens have not been the poetical inspiration he had hoped for!

You can connect with me on:

🌐 https://grjordan.com
🔲 https://facebook.com/carpetlessleprechaun

Subscribe to my newsletter:

✉ https://bit.ly/PatrickSmythe

Also by G R Jordan

G R Jordan writes across multiple genres including crime, dark and action adventure fantasy, feel good fantasy, mystery thriller and horror fantasy. Below is a selection of his work. Whilst all books are available across online stores, signed copies are available at his personal shop.

A Common Man - Inferno Book 2
Removed from his post and cast aside by his superiors. Without authority and any resources to call to hand. Can Macleod operate from the dark and hunt down the mysterious group before another child dies?

Having been sidelined from the investigation and fast tracked for an early retirement, DI Macleod knows that the child killer is still on the loose. With the assistance of his injured Colleague, DS Urquhart, Macleod finds himself operating beyond the law for the first time in his career. With DS McGrath increasingly frustrated by the glory hunting DCI, Macleod must pull whatever resources he can to bring about the arrest of the dark band of brothers before another innocent suffers.

With Hope removed, you need a rottweiler at your heels!

A Sweeping Darkness - Inferno Book 3
The public weeps as the killings begin again. With the chase now on, agendas are quickly accelerated. Can Macleod and McGrath pull together a ragged investigation to stop an unholy sacrifice?

Reinstated but still under the public glare, DI Macleod knows that the dark cult responsible for the first deaths are now feeling the pressure. Tales of brutality and sacrifice run rife leaving Macleod to sort rumour from reality. As the true nature of what the cult intends to do comes to light, Seoras and Hope find themselves in a desperate race to find missing children and Ross's adopted child.

For the love of God, he has to find them!

A Personal Favour (A Kirsten Stewart Thriller #9)

https://grjordan.com/product/a-personal-favour

A friend's daughter goes missing when reporting for a local paper. A town on the up but with a history steeped in blood. Can Kirsten break the steely cocoon of silence and find the girl before she is another tragic story?

Dealing with the desperate change in their circumstances, Craig receives a plea from an old friend to find his missing daughter. Being in no shape to assist, Kirsten takes his place and finds herself in a cold wilderness that lacks a warm welcome. When she digs too deep into the past, a desperate town seals itself off, leaving Kirsten trapped within.

Some stories are just too personal for the public to hear!

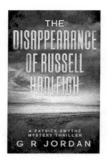

The Disappearance of Russell Hadleigh (Patrick Smythe Book 1)

https://grjordan.com/product/the-disappearance-of-russell-hadleigh

A retired judge fails to meet his golf partner. His wife calls for help while running a fantasy play ring. When Russians start co-opting into a fairly-traded clothing brand, can Paddy untangle the strands before the bodies start littering the golf course?

In his first full novel, Patrick Smythe, the single-armed former policeman, must infiltrate the golfing social scene to discover the fate of his client's husband. Assisted by a young starlet of the greens, Paddy tries to understand just who bears a grudge and who likes to play in the rough, culminating in a high stakes showdown where lives are hanging by the reaction of a moment. If you love pacey action, suspicious motives and devious characters, then Paddy Smythe operates amongst your kind of people.

Love is a matter of taste but money always demands more of its suitor.